DISNEP
THE SORCERER'S APPRENTICE

A novel based on the major motion picture

Adapted by James Ponti

Based on the screenplay by Doug Miro & Carlo Bernard and Matt Lopez

Screen Story by Matt Lopez and Lawrence Konner & Mark Rosenthal

Produced by Jerry Bruckheimer

Directed by Jon Turteltaub

DISNEP PRESS

NEW YORK

Printed in the United States of America
First Edition
1 3 5 7 9 10 8 6 4 2
J689-1817-1-10105
Library of Congress Catalog Card Number on file.
ISBN 978-1-4231-2690-4

Book design by Alfred Giuliani

Visit www.disneybooks.com

PROLOGUE

In all of history, there has been one sorcerer with more power than all who came before or after. This man was Merlin. He believed that magic was only to be used for the good of mankind. But his most trusted student, Morgana, did not share this belief. Her need for power exceeded all else. When he refused to help her in her quest to become stronger, she killed him.

With his dying breath, Merlin cast a spell over his apprentices—the three people chosen to carry out his ideal of magic. The spell would keep them from aging until they were able to find his rightful heir—the one sorcerer strong enough to inherit his ring and his incredible power. The Prime Merlinian.

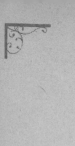

CHAPTER ONE

This story begins, as all great stories do, with a rather unassuming event at Bowling Green Park, the oldest public park in the great city of New York.

It was Dave Stutler's tenth birthday. He figured, now that he'd reached double digits, it was time to face his ultimate fear and tell Becky Barnes that he loved her. True, he was, well, a dork, and Becky, was, well, popular, but true love ran deep—or so his mother told him.

Their fourth-grade class had ventured into the city on a field trip and were now having lunch in the park. Dave had already blown a golden opportunity to talk to Becky during the ride into the city. He had drawn a picture of King Kong on the window of their school bus so that when they passed the Empire State Building, the picture looked like it was actually climbing the skyscraper.

"I really like your picture, Dave," Becky told him.

Unfortunately, Dave had been too shy to say anything. He only managed a nod, and just like that the conversation was over.

Now, though, he was ready.

Sort of.

He still didn't have the courage to talk to Becky. But he had written a note. It read, "Please check one. I would like to be Dave's . . ." Beneath that, there were two boxes: one marked FRIEND and one marked GIRLFRIEND. He snuck the note into her lunch bag.

Becky opened the bag. Her expression grew curious when she saw the note. Dave watched nervously as she read it, checked a box, and placed the note next to the fountain in the center of the park. Quickly, he walked over. But just as he reached the fountain, a huge gust of wind swooped through the park and carried the note out onto the sidewalk.

Dave chased after it, but each time he reached to grab the note, something sent it in a different direction. First it stuck to the wheel of a messenger bike. Then it got stuck to the paw of a poodle that was jogging with its owner. All the while, Dave kept chasing and chasing. He was so focused on the note he didn't realize he was straying out of the park and beyond the boundaries set by Ms. Algar, his teacher.

He finally "trapped" the note in an alleyway. The paper came to rest on the ground in front of an ancient-looking store. Then, out of nowhere, another gust of wind sucked the note up and through the store's mail slot!

Dave couldn't believe his eyes. He looked up at the ornate writing chiseled on the door:

ARCANA CABANA

ANTIQUITIES, OBSCURITIES, UNUSUAL GIFTS

BALTHAZAR BLAKE—PROPRIETOR

BY APPOINTMENT ONLY

Dave didn't have an appointment, but he was not about to leave without finding out which box Becky checked. He stepped into the shop and quickly decided the sign's use of the word *unusual* was an understatement. The dimly lit store was filled to the brim with bizarre-looking objects. Little statues and exotic pieces of art lined dusty shelves. One wall was covered with medieval weapons, and a bookshelf was filled with huge, dusty volumes in languages Dave didn't recognize. In one corner, he saw what looked like the skull of a . . . unicorn?

Following the narrow path that led through the store, Dave searched for the note. He couldn't shake the feeling that someone was watching him. He spun around and found himself face-to-face—with an ancient Incan mummy.

He let out a scream and knocked over a pyramid of antique marbles, sending them clattering across the floor. He jumped back and bumped into a bookcase, knocking over an antique bust that fell and shattered. The chain reaction continued, causing a large Chinese urn to tumble off its pedestal. Just as it was about to hit the ground, a hand reached out from the darkness and grabbed it.

Trembling with fear, Dave looked up. The hand belonged to a man who looked as unusual as the objects in the store. His eyes and hair were wild, and he wore a long dark coat. He had rings on every finger and weird-looking shoes on his feet. His movements were calm, yet powerful. This, Dave had to assume, was Balthazar Blake, the owner.

"Do you know what this is?" he asked angrily as he placed the urn back on the shelf.

Too scared to talk, Dave just shook his head no.

"The second emperor of the Han dynasty locked his least-favorite wife in this urn for ten years. To the day." Balthazar paused to make sure Dave grasped the danger involved. "They say you open it up, same thing will happen to you."

Dave was definitely weirded out. "I'm sorry," he stammered. "I was just looking for this note."

Balthazar cocked his head to one side, suddenly curious. "A note?"

"To a girl. It blew into your store. It was just a . . ."

Dave tried to think of the right word.

"*Coincidence?*" Balthazar offered.

"Yeah," Dave replied with a relieved smile.

Balthazar's eyes narrowed. He did not believe much in the concept of coincidence. He was much older than he appeared, and his many years of experience had taught him that most everything happened for a reason. Now he studied Dave carefully, wondering what might have brought this young man to his store.

"Can't beat a good coincidence," Balthazar said, friendlier than before. Dave wasn't sure which of the older man's moods was scarier. The store owner started digging through an overflowing drawer. "I have something I'd like to show you."

Balthazar pulled a slender mahogany case out of the drawer and placed it on the counter. He opened it to reveal a dragon figurine.

"This is very special," Balthazar said. "And if it likes you . . . you can keep it."

"I better not," Dave said quietly. "My teacher told me I couldn't stay long. She knows I'm here."

"You're a bad liar, Dave."

Wait a minute. How did the man know his name? Dave needed to get out . . . and fast. He raced toward the exit. But the door slammed shut and the latch slid into the locked position . . . all by itself.

Dave couldn't believe his eyes. He turned to face Blake. "Did you just . . ." He pointed back at the door.

"Did I what?" Balthazar asked calmly, acting as though nothing at all unusual was happening.

He held out the dragon for Dave to see.

"Do you see the inscription?"

Since he was obviously going nowhere, Dave took the dragon. He read the inscription aloud: "'*Take me up. Cast me away.*'" Suddenly, the dragon's tail and claws flickered to life. The creature crawled across the back of Dave's hand and wrapped itself around his finger. As Dave watched, the dragon turned into a ring, its eyes casting an eerie glow.

Balthazar smiled mysteriously. "I've been searching a long time and all over the world for you."

"For me?" Dave squeaked.

Balthazar nodded. "And, magically, here you are. That ring on your finger means something. It means you're going to be a very important sorcerer one day."

"A sorcerer!" Dave cried. What was this loony man talking about? He tried to catch his breath.

"But for now," Balthazar went on, "you are my apprentice. There is a lot to learn, and your first lesson begins now with your very own Encantus."

Dave wanted all of this to stop; he wanted to get back to his class and forget everything; he wanted to find that stupid note! But Balthazar was happily headed toward the back of the store, and the door was still locked.

"Don't move," he warned Dave. "*Don't touch anything.* I have eyes in the back of my head."

Dave laughed nervously. "Not moving," he called out, trying to reassure Balthazar and himself.

Suddenly, something started banging on the wall behind him from the other side, as if it was trying to get in. The banging grew louder and louder. Then, a hole formed in the wall, and an object flew out of it and right at Dave's head. He ducked at the very last moment.

Dave picked up the object. It appeared to be a

wooden nesting doll with a man wearing a top hat painted on its outermost layer. The dragon ring began to pulse with green light. Suddenly, glowing ripples of energy passed from the ring and wrapped around the doll. Dave felt a tingling in his hand and noticed a seam start to appear across the doll's surface.

He dropped it, just as a stream of cockroaches started pouring out through the seam. Then, as Dave watched in disbelief, the bugs transformed into the man from the outside of the doll.

This was Maxim Horvath. One of the most evil sorcerers ever to walk the earth was now free! He wore a top hat and suit and clenched a green crystal-topped cane in his fist.

"When am I?" demanded Horvath.

Dave stammered for a moment. "New . . . New York City!"

"I said WHEN! The year!" Horvath wailed, angrily waving his cane as he moved toward Dave.

Suddenly an unseen force seemed to grab Horvath and throw him up against the ceiling. Balthazar had returned. In one hand he carried a giant book. The other hand pointed at the sorcerer, who was pinned to the ceiling. He looked at Dave. "What happened to '*don't touch anything*'?"

Horvath struggled to break free. "Not very sporting, Balthazar!" he complained. "I hardly got a chance to stretch my legs."

"Be quiet!" Balthazar barked. He turned to Dave and tried to sound reassuring. "It's not you. He's been this way for a thousand years. For future reference, *apprentice* means you follow my instructions. Now where's the doll?"

Dave nodded in the doll's direction.

When Balthazar reached for the doll, Horvath used his cane to fire a bolt of energy at him.

As Balthazar flew through the air and slammed into a table, Horvath broke free of the spell that had him pinned to the ceiling. When the dust cleared, they were both standing and ready to resume a war that had clearly been raging for quite some time.

The two sorcerers began a battle that was like nothing Dave had ever seen before. They cast spells, chanted incantations, and practically caused a tornado in the middle of the shop. The objects that lined the shelves were now flying around like missiles.

"I'll have that doll," Horvath yelled as he grabbed a medieval sword from the wall. "My associates are eager to take in the sights."

"You and your Morganian buddies can't play nice, so I have to make you sit in the corner," Balthazar said as he pulled the horn off what was, indeed, a unicorn skull and used it to have a sword fight with Horvath. "No one's getting out of the Grimhold."

"The world belongs to us, Balthazar," Horvath hissed.

They both dived for the doll which sent it skittering across the floor to land right at Dave's feet.

"Dave, get out of here!" warned Balthazar. "Run!"

But Dave was paralyzed by fear. He didn't run. He just stood perfectly still, as a storm of objects—clocks, vases, the Incan mummy—flew past him, all the while telling himself, "This isn't happening."

Finally he noticed the Grimhold, as Balthazar called it, at his feet. He grabbed it and ran for the door. Just as he was about to get out, an unseen force started pulling him back. It was Horvath, who had somehow magically grabbed on to his backpack.

Papers flew out of the backpack and swirled around the room. Dave struggled and strained, trying to reach the door. But the pull was too strong.

Balthazar knew there was no other choice. He had found his apprentice, but if Horvath got his hands on the Grimhold it wouldn't matter—the world would be in grave danger. Frantically, his eyes searched the room until they spotted the one thing that could prevent—or at least delay—this disaster. Grabbing the Chinese urn, Balthazar opened it. Suddenly, he and Horvath were being sucked into the urn as if it were a giant vacuum. As he disappeared, Balthazar called out to Dave: "That Grimhold contains forces of evil. You've got to keep it safe!"

Right then, a giant sphere of light rocked the shop and knocked Dave into the wall. When he opened his eyes, he was all alone. There was no sign of Balthazar or Horvath.

Dave sprinted into the alley and realized he was still holding the doll. Despite Balthazar's words, Dave didn't want anything to do with it. He dropped it.

"David Stutler!" a voice commanded. "Don't *ever* leave your group without permission!"

Dave looked up to see his teacher and the entire class—including Becky Barnes—staring at him.

"There are these crazy wizard guys in there," he cried. "They're made out of roaches! They'll kill you!"

The students burst into laughter as Ms. Algar frowned and shook her head. Humoring him, she walked to the door to look inside.

"No," Dave pleaded. "Things come alive in there!"

But when Ms. Algar opened the door, the shop had returned to normal. Nothing looked out of place at all.

As bad as it was, it got worse.

"He peed his pants!" one of his classmates shouted.

Dave looked down and saw a dark stain on his pants. Soon all of the kids were laughing and pointing. Dave just stood there, horrified. He would never be able to live this down. It was the worst birthday ever.

He was much too upset to notice the nesting doll roll down the alley and into a gutter. He probably wouldn't have cared anyway. Dave wanted nothing to do with that shop—ever again.

CHAPTER TWO

The morning sun began to filter through the Manhattan skyline and suddenly New York City came to life. In a high-rise apartment, a woman dusted the Chinese urn that, unbeknownst to her, imprisoned two of the most powerful sorcerers of all time—Balthazar Blake and Maxim Horvath.

The woman's husband looked up from his newspaper and shook his head. "Why'd you buy that thing?"

"It's an antique!" she told him.

"It's junk!" the man said, turning back to his paper.

It was a recurring argument, and as usual she ignored him and returned to her dusting. But neither of them noticed what happened a few minutes later as the first shaft of morning light reached the urn.

The urn began to vibrate, ever so slightly.

It had been ten years. To the day.

In another part of Manhattan, Dave Stutler was blissfully asleep, unaware of any danger. Dave was still shy and nerdy, just older. A sophomore at New York University, Dave didn't have much of a social life. His only friend was his roommate, Bennett. But despite Bennett's best efforts to get Dave out to parties and clubs, he preferred working in his physics lab.

On the morning of his twentieth birthday, Dave got his first present the moment he woke up. The "gift" was a giant string of drool dangling from the mouth of the bulldog that had climbed up onto his chest. The dog's name was Tank, and he belonged to Bennett.

Dave swatted away the drool, picked up Tank, and carried him into the living room where Bennett was eating cereal and watching ESPN.

"I like Tank and all," Dave said as he placed the dog down next to his roommate. "But the drooling thing, it's not cool."

"He likes you, if it's any consolation," Bennett said as he slurped a spoonful of cereal. "Happy birthday, by the way." He tossed Dave a snack pack of cookies. "You're up early," Bennett observed.

"Professor Heiderman asked me to give a presentation to his Physics 101 class."

"Teaching English majors to do long division?" Bennett said, deadpan.

Dave gave him a don't-you-realize-how-important-this-is look. "It's Heiderman's class. If I want the Newton scholarship, I'm going to need his recommendation."

"What you *need* is a night out," Bennett declared mid–cereal chomp. Since moving in with Dave, he'd heard way too much about work and seen way too little in terms of fun. He eyed his roommate now— tall, skinny, his dark hair sticking out in all directions. He looked every bit the mad genius.

"I've got to get my project done," Dave said, ignoring Bennett's suggestion.

"Dave, are you familiar with the gray wolf?" Bennett said as he placed his cereal bowl on the coffee table and pointed to the wildlife calendar on the wall.

"Please, not this again," Dave pleaded.

"The gray wolf's a pack animal, but within the pack he must contribute. He must hunt and grunt. He must *participate*!"

Dave rolled his eyes. He'd heard this all before.

"You can't be afraid to live life!" Bennett exclaimed. "You'll end up booted from the pack. Alone."

Luckily, the phone rang and Dave was saved from further lecture. Leaving Bennett to talk to his mom over the phone about *American Idol*, Dave grabbed his coat and headed to class.

As Dave hurried across Washington Square Park to the physics building, his hair got in his eyes and he chidded himself for not wearing more layers. By the time he got to Meyer Hall, the morning chill was just lifting. He slipped into the back row of Professor Heiderman's classroom and scanned his notes one last time.

Suddenly, a gust of wind blew in through an open door and sent a page of his notes fluttering into the air. Dave chased it down the aisle. Whenever he got close, something carried it away. Finally, he managed to grab the page by diving across the floor.

"Everything okay down there?" a voice asked.

Dave looked up. Then he looked right back down. Then up. He couldn't believe his eyes. Standing over him was a gorgeous girl. She had sparkling blue eyes that he recognized in an instant.

"Becky? Becky Barnes?"

She looked at him blankly.

"We were in fourth grade together," Dave pressed. "Actually, kindergarten through fourth grade."

Becky's eyes widened. "Wait a second. You were *that* kid. Dave Stutler. That place, what was it called?"

Dave slumped. "Arcana Cabana," he said, wishing she had recalled something other than the worst moment of his life.

"I totally remember that day," she said. "It's like one of those permanent childhood memories."

Exactly what Dave was afraid of. "Glad I made the cut," he mumbled.

Becky smiled and nodded as more of the memory came back to her. "You transferred or something, right?"

"I did indeed," Dave replied, wishing he could

vanish into thin air now. "Transferred and got some help. Turns out it was all the result of a glucose imbalance. Hallucinations aren't uncommon in young subjects."

Becky cringed. "And I remember your pants were completely . . ."

"So, you're taking this class," Dave interrupted, hoping to change the topic. This trip down memory lane had already been painful enough.

Luckily, Professor Heiderman walked into the room at that moment.

"Morning, everyone," the professor said.

He motioned toward Dave. "Mr. Stutler's here to give a no doubt dazzling demonstration of conductivity." His sarcasm was not lost on the class, who all chuckled.

Dave awkwardly took his spot at the demonstration table where he had set up his experiment. The previous evening, a clear Plexiglas box that held a small device and a baseball had been placed on the table.

"To illustrate the aforementioned conductivity," Dave said, trying to sound like a professor, "we're going to scorch the outer surface off this baseball using an electric field generated by this little bad boy known as a Tesla coil."

Dave turned up the power supply, and a bolt of electricity suddenly crackled from the coil to the ball. The students were startled. The ball didn't react at all.

"Problem is, the ball is highly resistive," Dave explained. "Our reaction will increase if we douse the ball in water." He dunked the ball in a bowl of water. "The salt ions in the water will act as a conductor," he continued.

Dave looked at his audience. He knew that he should be trying to impress the professor, but catching Becky's eye, he had a sudden impulse to impress *her*. Unfortunately, at the moment she looked bored. Dave decided to up the coolness factor.

"Let's get it bumpin'!" he said as he turned up the voltage. A few kids in the class laughed. More groaned.

Dave was getting agitated. Not only was he failing to be cool, but his experiment was failing, too. Even though a bolt of electricity was continually zapping it, the ball was hardly reacting.

Flustered, Dave turned up the power as high as it would go. Within seconds, the box began to fill up with smoke and the ball began vibrating wildly.

The professor tried to interject. "Perhaps you should just—"

It was too late. With a bang, the ball exploded and a mess of cork flew out over the class. There was a long silence as Dave looked at everyone in total disbelief. Then the class erupted into a round of applause. This was the most fun they'd had in physics all semester.

Professor Heiderman, however, was not pleased.

Dave didn't even have a chance to explain. At that moment the bell rang, and the students quickly packed up and headed for the doors.

"Don't forget, midterm next week," the professor called out as they exited.

Dave wasn't going to stick around either. Noticing that Becky was leaving, he decided to take a chance. Books clutched in his hands, he chased after her and caught up to her in front of the building.

"Hey, Becky," Dave said loud enough to be heard over her earphones. She nodded hi and they fell into step. Walking alongside her, Dave tried to start a conversation. "I don't know if you've heard of it, but I'm a candidate for the Newton Scholarship."

He hoped that sounded impressive.

"Nice," she said, hardly interested.

"Winner studies in London," he continued. "Heiderman's on the committee, so that back there . . ."

"Wasn't good?" she finished.

Dave shook his head. They continued walking in silence, Dave desperately trying to think of something to say. "You're interested in physics?" he asked finally.

"I'm interested in graduating."

"So, it's a requirement situation, huh?"

Becky nodded. "My brain just doesn't think physics," she said. "Midterm next week will be a nightmare."

"What does it think?" Dave asked. "Your brain."

"Music. Mostly." Then she told him she was an English and prelaw major, parents choice, not hers. She stopped speaking when they arrived in front of the communications building. "This is me," she said, motioning to the stairs leading down to the basement. A sticker on the door read, WNYU.

"You work at the radio station?" Dave asked.

"I do a show in the afternoons," she answered. "It's just college radio. There's, like, seven people listening."

"I'll listen." Dave said. "Round it up to eight."

Becky smiled, suddenly seeing Dave as more than just a dork. He was kind of . . . funny.

"Eight is the only Fibonacci number that's a perfect cube," he added.

Or not.

"What kind of music do you play?" he asked.

Becky's face lit up as she began to talk about music. "Mostly low-fi. Old vinyl if I can find it. Weird stuff. Anything that makes me feel something—you know—that I didn't expect to."

"That's cool," Dave said, wishing he knew what she was talking about. But he didn't really know anything about music.

"Anyway, nice to see you again," she said, clearly wanting to get inside. "Good luck with your scholarship."

But just as she was about to go into the radio station, a bolt of lightning crackled and struck the giant antenna on top of the building. The metal rod flashed for a moment and then started smoking.

Becky's shoulders slumped. "I think that's our antenna," she said.

Dave smiled. He had an idea.

Across town, another type of storm was brewing in the high-rise apartment. The Chinese urn was no longer just trembling, it was shaking violently. As the woman reached to grab it, the top flew off and slammed into the ceiling. A cloud of smoke filled the room. When it cleared, a dark figure was hunched on the floor.

It was Maxim Horvath.

"Am I out first?" he demanded.

In answer, the woman fainted.

Horvath checked for any sign of Balthazar. Seeing none, he grabbed the urn and headed out to the balcony. "Our ten years are up, Balthazar!" he cried gleefully. "I'll tell the kid you said 'hello.'"

With that, Horvath tossed the urn off the balcony

and left the apartment. But perhaps he had been too hasty. A few stories before it hit the ground, a second plume of smoke poured out of the urn. From out of the smoke came a hand that grabbed the railing of a third-story balcony. The hand belonged to Balthazar. Holding on tightly, he let out a deep sigh as the urn shattered on the sidewalk below. By the time the pedestrians looked up to see what was going on, Balthazar was already gone.

Once again, Dave was unaware of any impending danger. He was too busy helping Becky. At that moment, he was in the WNYU radio station, trying to fix a transmitter panel in the control room. The lightning had fried the entire system. Luckily, Dave knew his way around circuits and electricity.

Watching him were Becky and her friend and fellow DJ, Andre. Dave didn't know what to make of Andre. He was hip, looked like a model, and seemed to know music as well as she did. Dave was worried that he was Becky's boyfriend. But he tried to block that out and focus on the electronics.

"Good news," he said, "you're still transmitting. Bad news, your return loss is way too low."

Becky gave him a look of total confusion.

"I work with a lot of transducers," he explained.

"Sorry," she said, still looking confused. "Science word."

"Right. A transducer converts one form of energy into another. Your antenna takes electrical energy and converts it into electromagnetic energy in the form of radio waves," Dave explained.

Once again, Becky looked lost.

"Am I geeking you out?" he asked.

"Little bit," she said with a smile that said it was all right.

"Yeah," Andre added snarkily. "*No hablo* nerd."

Ignoring him, Dave adjusted some knobs and smiled as music suddenly filled the room,

"We're transducing!" Becky exclaimed happily, speaking nerd for the moment.

Dave smiled at her and then motioned to the radio equipment. "This is pretty important to you, huh?"

"My show is like the one thing . . ." She stopped

midsentence, not wanting to reveal too much. "You know what I mean?"

"Yeah," Dave nodded. He knew exactly what she meant. "Physics."

They shared a smile.

"I'll see you around," Dave said.

Becky laughed. "Careful. Seems like stuff tends to blow up around you."

Dave wanted to say something more. But he was too nervous. He froze, just as he had on the school bus during their field trip. Then Andre put his arm around Becky and gave her a kiss on the cheek.

Dave sighed. Always the right place, but always the wrong time.

CHAPTER THREE

D eep beneath the city, NYU had allowed Dave to convert an abandoned subway platform into a modest physics lab. Its mix of outdated equipment and secondhand furniture wasn't much to look at, but the protection and privacy that came with being so far underground made it ideal for Dave's high-voltage experiments. It had become Dave's home away from home—and Bennett's.

After his disastrous encounter with Becky, Dave had immediately headed to the lab. Now, he tinkered with two giant Tesla coils while his roommate kicked back on an old sofa and grilled him about Becky.

"You just left?"

"That's not the point," Dave replied as he tightened a coil. "I *fixed* the antenna. I *made* an impression. She will definitely remember me!"

"Seriously? You didn't ask her out? You just 'fixed her antenna' and left?"

Dave considered this for a moment. "I thought about asking her out. Thought *seriously* about it."

Bennett stood up and walked over to his roommate. He put an arm around Dave's shoulder. "Think *seriously* about hooking up some self-confidence," he advised.

Dave ran a hand through his hair and sighed. "I missed my chance with this girl ten years ago."

"Hey, maybe you'll get another shot with her," Bennett said with a smile. Then he added, "in ten years."

Dave's shoulders slumped.

His message delivered, Bennett put on his coat. He looked over at the two large columns that supported the Tesla coils. "You really think these old-school bad boys are going to win you the Newton?"

"You won't be laughing when I create sustainable plasma," Dave said by way of an answer.

"True. Nothing funny about sustainable plasma." Bennett headed for the door. "Last chance to observe the effect of liquids contained in a cold glass."

Dave shook his head.

Expecting that response, Bennett shrugged and walked out, leaving Dave alone with his devices.

Stepping up to the coils control panel, located in a safety cage, Dave threw a switch.

Long tendrils of high-voltage electricity began to leap from one Tesla coil to the other. They cast a glow over the room and brought a smile to Dave's face. For the first time that day, he felt good. It was here in the physics lab that he actually had self-confidence. He turned on the radio and tuned it to the college station.

He heard Becky talking over the airwaves. "Maybe it's just me," she said, "but I can't get this next song out of my head."

Some funky song he'd never heard before started playing. She may not have had a ton of listeners, but Becky now had one who was extremely devoted. Dave turned up the volume and went back to work.

* * *

When it opened in 1930, the Chrysler Building was the tallest in the world. This record was beaten eleven months later by the Empire State Building and since then by many others. But, while other skyscrapers had surpassed its impressive height, few, if any, had ever managed to match its magnificent blend of art and architecture.

The sixty-first floor is home to the most famous example of that blend—a collection of stainless-steel eagle gargoyles that look over Manhattan. And it was here that Balthazar Blake came to survey the city after his ten-year confinement.

Looking out over the city, his eyes in shadow under his hat and his long trench coat flapping in the wind, the sorcerer was both worried and hopeful. He was worried about the chaos that the likes of Maxim Horvath could wreak by unleashing his fellow sorcerers from their Grimhold prison. And he was hopeful that Dave Stutler might help him fight it.

As he gently stroked a glimmering eagle, one of his rings began to glow. Yes, he thought, this was hopeful indeed.

* * *

Dave was still humming the song from the radio later that evening when he walked into his apartment and headed straight for the refrigerator. He was going to treat himself to a chocolate soda. But then he noticed something unusual on the refrigerator door—a book report he had written in the fourth grade.

How had that gotten there?

Suddenly a deep voice spoke out from behind him. "I thought the B-minus was generous."

Dave spun around and found Maxim Horvath, sitting with his feet on the kitchen table and his hands clasped behind his head.

"Boo," said Horvath.

Dave screamed.

"Where's the Grimhold?" he demanded, standing up and calmly approaching Dave.

Dave stumbled backward as he stammered, "I-I don't know what you . . ."

"You are David Stutler?" Horvath asked. "From Ms. Algar's fourth-grade class."

"I am," Dave answered. "I mean, I was."

Horvath moved closer. "That doll held something very powerful," he said. "Something very important to me. And you had it last. I want it back."

"Here's the thing," Dave said. "You're not here, okay?"

Horvath looked perplexed. "Excuse me?"

Dave thought back to what the doctors told him after the incident at the Arcana Cabana. "No offense. But you're just a hallucination, and I need some sugar. It's a glucose thing."

Dave fumbled with the chocolate soda as he tried to unscrew the top. Opening it, he closed his eyes and took a long, cold swig, hoping that the sugar would somehow solve his "glucose" problem. It didn't work.

"You're still here."

"I've been released from a ten-year sentence during which my only reading material was your so-called report on 'The Life of Napoleon Bonaparte'," Horvath stated, ignoring Dave's odd behavior. "Your analysis was obvious. Your prose was weak."

"I was nine," Dave reminded him.

"I knew the man. You missed his essence completely," Horvath told him. "Where is the Grimhold?"

"I'm telling you, I don't have it," Dave said.

Horvath flashed an evil smile. "I'll cut the truth out of you."

Dave was not about to wait around for that. He shoved past Horvath, sprinted through the door and down the hall toward the elevator.

Horvath rolled his eyes and calmly walked toward the hallway. He saw the calendar on the wall featuring pictures of gray wolves. Horvath waved a finger, and the wolves from the calendar came alive and instantly began chasing after Dave.

Looking over his shoulder, Dave saw the pursuing pack. He frantically pushed the elevator button a few more times. Nothing happened. He gave up and ran down the stairs. The wolves followed him until he managed to run out the front door and slam it shut before they could get out.

Dave wanted to put as much distance as possible between himself and those wolves. He sprinted to the elevated train platform. But all too quickly, the wolves had gotten free.

There was no train in sight when he reached the platform, so he started to run down the tracks, the wolves right behind him. Suddenly, he tripped and fell to the ground. Looking up, he saw the wolves, ready to attack, just waiting for the final order from Horvath, who had also reached them.

"Please, don't," Dave pleaded.

Horvath considered for a moment and shrugged. He signaled the wolves to attack.

The wild animals charged. Dave threw his hands up in front of his face, prepared for pain. But nothing happened. Instead, the air was suddenly filled with the sounds of soft squeaks. Opening his eyes, Dave's mouth dropped. The wolves had been transformed into harmless, cuddly puppies.

What was going on?

Horvath was fuming. He had a very good idea of what was going on. He looked up toward the sky just as a giant steel wing slammed into him. It was the eagle from the Chrysler building. It was alive—

and being ridden by Balthazar Blake.

"No way," Dave said as he stared at the unbelievable creature hovering right in front of him.

"You got tall," Balthazar said.

Dave screamed.

Horvath jumped up and cocked his crystal-headed cane, ready to throw a spell. But Balthazar saw it coming and cast a temporal-displacement spell on Horvath. The spell slowed Horvath down to one-twentieth of his normal speed.

"Where's the doll?" Balthazar asked, turning back to Dave.

Dave tried to answer, but what came out was just unintelligible stammering.

Balthazar shook his head. He didn't have time for this. "All right, get up here." He motioned to the slow-moving Horvath. "That speed bump's not going to last forever."

"I'm scared of flying!" Dave protested. "On *planes!*"

"Well, it's your lucky day," Balthazar said with a wry smile. "I brought an eagle."

Before he could say another word, Balthazar

hoisted Dave up and onto the bird. Moments later, they were flying above the city.

Dave's mind was racing. None of this was possible. As a scientist, he knew exactly *how* it wasn't possible. But, somehow, it *was* happening. And, somehow, he was landing on the sixty-first floor of the Chrysler Building on a stainless-steel eagle. Balthazar dismounted the eagle and landed smoothly on the observation deck. Dave was less smooth. He basically just fell to the ground.

"So, Dave," Balthazar said, "ten years, huh? How's adulthood treating you?"

They were making cheery chit-chat? No way. "What you just did!" Dave cried, "it's *not* possible! There are laws. Laws of physics."

"Everything we do is well within the laws of physics. You just don't know all the laws yet," Balthazar said as though that was the most obvious answer in the world.

"I assume from your reaction back there you lost the Grimhold," Balthazar went on. "Which happens to hold the greatest evil that man has ever known. We've got to find the doll before *he* does."

Dave flashed him a look. "*We?*"

Balthazar kept going along as if all of this was reasonable. "Dave, you could be a Merlinean. A powerful sorcerer."

"Hang on," Dave replied. "A Merlinean what?"

Balthazar tried to explain. "Merlineans believe magic should be used to *help* man. Morganians believe it should be used to *rule* him. We've been fighting for centuries. I'm the last Merlinean," he said, sounding almost sad.

"None of this makes sense," Dave said, repeating what he'd been thinking since the wolves came to life.

"You just rode on a steel eagle," Balthazar said with a wry smile. "Think it's time to put skepticism in check?"

The dude had a point. He nodded.

"The doll's called the Grimhold," Balthazar continued, aware that he was slowly getting through to the young man. "It's a prison for the most dangerous Morganians, each one locked up in a layer of the doll. Horvath, for reasons relating to his poor character, wants to free his fellow Morganians. That can't happen."

Dave shook his head. "You're not doing this to me. Not again. Do you have any idea what my life's been like for the last ten years?"

"I've been stuck in an urn for the last ten years," Balthazar pointed out.

"So have I!" Dave yelled. Well, it wasn't an urn exactly. . . . "Ten years of kids making fun of me! Do you know in some parts of the tristate area they still call having a total freak-out breakdown '*doing a Stutler*?' Did you know that?"

"I did not," Balthazar said. "But the truth is you have a very special gift. You have to see that, believe in it."

"I don't care!" Dave said, raising his voice a little more than he intended. "I just want to forget about the Arcana Cabana. Forget about magic. Forget it all."

Dave waited for Balthazar to say something. But he didn't. He just kept looking at something in the distance. Focusing. Finally, he looked back at Dave and calmly said, "You should duck."

Dave turned just in time to see a large object heading right at him. At the last moment he ducked and fell to the ground. When he got up he saw the flying object that had landed right next to him. It was his bedroom dresser.

"You just wanted to forget Arcana Cabana, forget magic, right?" Balthazar asked.

Dave, too stunned to speak, nodded.

"Then let me ask you something." Balthazar opened the top drawer of the dresser and pulled out the dragon ring. "Why'd you keep the ring?"

Dave looked at him. He didn't have an answer.

"You want to forget what happened that day," Balthazar said. "But part of you wants to *believe*."

Balthazar held the ring out to Dave. The coiled dragon glimmered in the moonlight.

"I was going to sell that thing on eBay," Dave said not very convincingly. "Haven't gotten around to posting photos yet."

"You're still a bad liar, Dave. But I like that about you. It's a good sign. Magic exists. You have the gift."

"No," Dave said forcefully. "I have a life!"

"Which consists of what?"

"It consists of a girl who . . ." He didn't really

know what to say about Becky. "I'm trying to win a scholarship . . . and . . . I'm not a sorcerer, okay?"

"You're the last person Horvath saw with the Grimhold," Balthazar explained. "Not the kind of thing he just forgets. So, unless you want the highest GPA in the intensive-care unit, you better help me find the Grimhold before he does."

"This is crazy!" Dave shouted. He felt like a broken record.

Balthazar offered him a deal. "Help me get it back," he said, "and you're done. You can walk away."

Dave thought about it for a moment. He realized that Horvath would continue to haunt him until he got what he wanted. And he couldn't deal with the likes of those wolves again. They had a deal.

With a quick nod of his head, Balthazar looked out at the city. He held his hand over the skyline and closed his eyes.

"What are you doing?" Dave asked.

Balthazar didn't answer. But when he opened his eyes the sky had become perfectly clear—except for one lone rain cloud, hovering over the city.

"Looks like downtown, huh?" he said, motioning toward the cloud.

"Wait, what is that?" Dave asked.

"Sorcerer tracking device," Balthazar explained. "Biometric-pressure spell disrupts the atmosphere directly above it."

Dave shook his head in disbelief.

"I've been protecting the Grimhold from Horvath for nearly a thousand years," Balthazar said. "I've taken some precautions."

"A thousand years? How old are you?"

Balthazar shrugged. "Depends on which calendar you use."

They started toward the stairs. Dave stopped. "You'll put my dresser back, right?" he asked.

Balthazar nodded, and they started off on their adventure together. They had a Grimhold to retrieve, and that meant they needed some transportation.

CHAPTER FOUR

A chill wind whistled, and Dave zipped up his jacket to fight the cold. He and Balthazar had made their way inside the massive structure that served as the New York Police Department tow yard. The city kept the cars it impounded for parking violations in the big yard. So, for the ten years Balthazar had been locked in a Chinese urn, his car had been locked up here.

"We need to hurry," Balthazar whispered as they followed the attendant through the sea of cars. "If I can track the Grimhold, so can Horvath."

"Why don't we just take the eagle?" Dave asked.

"A little high profile, don't you think?" Balthazar said, raising an eyebrow.

Dave wondered what type of car a sorcerer actually drove. He couldn't picture Balthazar in a station wagon or compact. In fact, he couldn't picture him in any car.

Then they turned the corner.

Dave recognized it the moment he saw it. It was a 1935 Rolls-Royce Phantom. Even a science geek like him knew about this car. It was, without a doubt, one of the most luxurious cars ever manufactured. Just looking at him, Dave could tell Balthazar loved everything about the car, from its silver Flying Lady hood ornament to its sleek design to its powerful 7.7-liter, 30-horsepower, 6-cylinder engine.

Balthazar lovingly ran his hand along the hood. Even covered in ten years worth of dust, it was breathtaking.

"I'll call for a tow," the attendant said.

Balthazar looked up and smiled. "Won't be necessary."

The clerk laughed. There was no way the battery was still working. But even as the thought flashed across the clerk's mind, the car roared to life. Balthazar hadn't even gotten in yet.

"She missed me," he explained.

Dave looked over the car, its engine growling like a monster. "So *this* is low profile?"

They climbed in, and Balthazar started to snake his way out of the lot.

"This car's engine is the same used in the Spitfires and Mustangs that beat the Nazis," Balthazar said. "It's not a coincidence the engine that won World War Two was named the *Merlin*."

"It was designed by a sorcerer?" Dave asked, curious.

Balthazar nodded. "Merlineans protect man and guide his journey toward enlightenment. Penicillin, trial-by-jury, the microscope, lunar-lander."

It seemed as if the sorcerer would have gone on, but just then they pulled out of the lot and onto the street. Balthazar smiled and savored the moment as he floored the accelerator. The initial thrust was strong enough to push Dave back into his seat a bit.

"I'm going to give you the basics, strictly Sorcery 101," Balthazar explained, glancing at the rain cloud. "First, put on the ring."

Dave hesitated. He didn't have fond memories of the last time he wore it.

"Nothing's going to happen," Balthazar promised.

Dave slipped it on and Balthazar swerved the car.

"Kidding," he said, flashing what Dave assumed was a smile. "Sorcery is the ability to manipulate matter on a molecular level. That's the essence of magic."

"You're still kidding, right?"

Balthazar shook his head. "Ever heard how people only use ten percent of their brains? Well, more like eight-and-a-half percent. Sorcerers are able to manipulate matter because they're born with the capability to use the entire power of their brain. Which explains why molecular physics comes so easy to you."

Dave thought for a moment before asking, "So wait, is sorcery science or magic?"

"*Yes*," Balthazar replied without hesitation.

Just then, they turned onto a narrow street in Chinatown. Balthazar looked up at the cloud. They were getting close.

"For now, all you need is a basic combat spell—making fire."

Dave gave him a look of disbelief. "You want me to conjure flames out of thin air?"

Balthazar nodded. "What causes molecules to heat up?"

"They vibrate."

Balthazar nodded in the direction of a meter maid who was sliding a ticket under the windshield wiper of a parked car. This was going to be his demonstration.

"Step one, clear your mind. Step two, see the molecules. Step three, make them vibrate."

Balthazar stared intently at the parking ticket, and in a matter of seconds it burst into flames and incinerated. "Got it?"

"Are you joking?" Dave said in disbelief. "I definitely don't *got* it."

"Trust the ring," Balthazar said as he gave him a friendly pat on the shoulder. "Oh, and keep it subtle. Civilians can't know magic exists. That would be . . . complicated. Sorcery must *always* live in the shadows."

He stopped to concentrate on the road. A street festival was blocking the way, so they parked and continued on foot. The celebration was jammed with people and vendors. A group of performers made a giant paper dragon dance to the rhythm of live drum music.

As they rounded the corner they saw that it was raining—but only over one store, an acupuncturist's shop.

They had found the Grimhold.

"Wait here," Balthazar said as he waved a finger and stopped the rain. "Keep an eye out for Horvath."

"What do I do if I see him?"

"Step one, clear your mind. Step two"—Balthazar could tell by Dave's panicked look that he wasn't ready to cast any spells—"just scream."

With purposeful strides, Balthazar entered the shop. He quickly checked for any sign of the Grimhold, or of Horvath.

"Can I help you?" asked the old woman behind the counter.

"I'm looking for a nesting doll about so high," he said, holding his hands about nine inches apart. "Angry-looking Chinese gentleman on the front."

As she began to look on the shelf, Balthazar noticed

a butterfly flutter out from the shadows. Something about it caught his attention.

"*Neih hou ma?*" he said.

She turned and smiled. "Ah, you speak Mandarin?"

Balthazar returned the smile for a second—and then blasted the woman across the room. When she slammed into the wall, she transformed into Horvath.

"That was Cantonese," Balthazar said.

From where he sat, slumped on the floor, Horvath looked up at his rival. "You always were the linguist. You know, an old associate of mine speaks impeccable Cantonese."

Horvath lifted his coat and held up the Grimhold. Balthazar was too late. A layer had been opened. There was a burst of light, and the butterfly suddenly transformed into a menacing Chinese sorcerer with a spectacular dragon on his silk robe. His hair was shaved except for a ponytail that ran down the center. He looked young, angry, and in fighting shape. And instead of fingernails he had silver clawlike nails.

"You've met Sun Lok," Horvath explained. "In fact, you're the one who locked him in the Grimhold."

Sun Lok glared at Balthazar. There was no love lost here. Without hesitation, Sun Lok cast a spell. A flurry of acupuncture needles flew off the table and right at him. Balthazar ducked for cover, using the cape of his leather trench coat as a shield.

When the needles bounced off the coat, he waved his hands at Sun Lok and sent an energy bolt that blasted him through the shop window and onto the street. Sun Lok landed right at Dave's feet.

When Sun Lok got up, he noticed the dragon ring around Dave's finger. His eyes burned with anger.

"This?" Dave said, panicking as he pointed at his ring. "This is plastic, a toy. I'm just a bystander . . . civilian . . . innocent guy."

Balthazar leaned out through the shattered window. "Keep him occupied for a sec, okay, Dave."

Dave's mouth quickly dried out. "I don't know that guy," he said to Sun Lok. "Never seen him before."

Two separate battles began. There was one in the shop between Balthazar and Horvath and one on the street between Sun Lok and Dave. Inside, the sorcerers slipped in and out of the shadows, carefully stalking each other. Outside, things were less subtle.

As a Morganian, Sun Lok didn't care if civilians saw public displays of magic. Looking around for a weapon, Sun Lok's eyes landed on the paper parade dragon. Quickly, he cast a spell, turning it into a real one.

Dave gulped as the eight-legged creature sized him up as if he were dinner. Then he ran. The dragon chased after him.

Catching movement through the window, Balthazar saw what was happening and cast a blizzard of confetti over the crowd. It was so dense that no one could really see what was going on.

While Balthazar was distracted, Horvath grabbed a Chinese flag from the wall and started snapping it like a towel. With each snap, the yellow star on the flag shot off a new razor-sharp throwing star.

Balthazar was being pulled in two directions at once, dodging the throwing stars while scanning the confetti for Dave. He saw the dragon chase him into a barber shop and turned his attention back to Horvath.

Balthazar quickly cast a spell that stopped a

throwing star in midair. Then he motioned toward a beaded curtain which wrapped itself around Horvath. As the Morganian struggled to get free, the Grimhold fell from his hands and rolled across the floor.

With a wink at Horvath, Balthazar picked up the nesting doll and jumped out the window into the confetti storm.

He lifted his hands, and a tunnel formed in the confetti. This cleared a path for him to see that Dave had made it out of the shop and was now on a fire escape, the dragon closing in on him.

"See the molecules!" Balthazar called out.

Dave wanted to argue that this might not be the best time for a lesson, but he knew Balthazar would show little sympathy. So instead he focused on Sun Lok, who was directing the dragon from the ground, and made a spell-casting motion with his hands.

"Nothing's happening!" Dave exclaimed.

"You skipped the first step."

"The first step," Dave said as he ran through the hasty lesson in his mind. "Clear my mind!"

Dave looked at the approaching dragon and

thought clearing his mind was a little unreasonable.

"Are you insane?" he yelled at Balthazar.

Dave started climbing up the fire escape again, toward the roof of the building. The dragon followed him, its body slithering up the metal stairs.

Dave closed his eyes and did everything he could to clear his mind as the dragon got closer. Finally, just as the beast was about to strike, Dave opened his eyes and reached his hand toward Sun Lok.

"Fire!" Dave commanded.

Sun Lok looked down as the dragon embroidered on his robe burst into flames.

The same thing happened to the real dragon just as it reached the roof of the building. Then the flaming dragon fell off the roof—and crushed Sun Lok on the street below.

Inside the shop, Horvath freed himself from the curtain. Stepping out onto the street, he was just in time to see Dave up on the roof. His eyes focused on the green ring glowing brightly on Dave's finger.

"It can't be!" he exclaimed. This was significant.

Dave, however, was too excited to notice any

of this. He had just defeated a dragon and a great sorcerer with nothing more than his own magic powers. Powers! He couldn't get over it. He quickly climbed down the fire escape and jumped onto the street in front of Balthazar.

"Did you see that?" he said.

Balthazar grabbed him and quickly led him toward the Phantom. "No time for an end-zone dance."

As they walked, their clothes magically transformed into police uniforms. Just then, a pair of police cars pulled up and came to a screeching halt.

"Talk to me," a police captain said as he jumped out of one of the cars. "What happened?"

Balthazar answered, only now he had a New York accent. "Bottle rocket meets paper dragon in this festival here," he explained, motioning toward the sea of confusion behind them. "Lit it up like a birthday cake."

The police captain shook his head. "We got swamped with calls saying there was a real dragon."

Balthazar leaned in closer. "Between you and me,

Cap, I think some of these folks were hitting the sake pretty hard."

Dave interrupted. "Sake's Japanese, actually."

Balthazar shot him a look. "Pipe down, rookie!"

The captain looked out at the festival and back at Balthazar. He nodded, convinced that the people had been mistaken. Balthazar gave him a salute and led Dave back toward the car.

Once they got out of the captain's earshot, Balthazar gave him a look. "'Sake's Japanese'?!" he repeated sarcastically.

"Well, it is!" Dave answered.

"I was in character!"

As they walked, the reality of what had just happened hit Dave.

"Did you see what I did back there? I was, like"—Dave searched for the right word to describe it—"money back there. Double money. Money-money."

Balthazar tucked the Grimhold into his overcoat and put out his hand. "Just give me the ring back, money-money."

Suddenly, Dave remembered their deal. They

had agreed to a one-time thing.

"I'm a man of my word," Balthazar said. "You helped me. We're done."

It occurred to Dave that what had just happened had made him feel special. He wasn't sure if he wanted that feeling to go away. He looked down at the ring. "It's just, well, it feels pretty good on my finger."

Balthazar tried to play it cool. This was what he expected to happen, but he needed Dave to realize his destiny on his own.

"So, what are you saying, Dave?"

Dave thought long and hard. Then he looked right at Balthazar. Now there was a sparkle in his eye, like the one he got when he talked about physics.

"I want to know more."

Balthazar just nodded. "We'll need a place to work. Somewhere private, where Horvath can't find us."

Dave smiled. He knew the perfect place.

CHAPTER FIVE

The fluorescent lights hissed to life and lit up Dave's underground lab. Balthazar looked around and smiled. It *was* perfect.

"Used to be a subway turnaround," Dave explained. "NYU bought it back in the forties for atomic research. They put me in here, because some of my work isn't exactly . . . safe."

Balthazar studied the two large columns in the middle of the room.

Dave started to explain them. "Those are . . ."

"Tesla coils," Balthazar interrupted. "I'm so pleased. All these years you thought you were running away from sorcery. It's not a coincidence you built these electrical-field generators. Dave, *this* is your magic. Dr. Tesla was my friend and a great Merlinean."

Dave considered this for a moment. Maybe science and magic did intersect. Maybe this *was* all part of his destiny.

"I didn't get the chance to give you this before," Balthazar said, pulling out a tiny book no bigger than a book of matches. "Your Encantus."

Dave thought back to that day ten years earlier. "I remember it being bigger," he said.

Balthazar gave him a knowing nod. "Pocket edition," he said as he began unfolding the book, one hand over the other. Each time he turned a page, the book grew bigger. Within a few moments it was huge. "The Encantus is your textbook: the art and science and history of sorcery. Including our recent history."

As proof, he opened it to the last page. There in vivid color were images from the Arcana Cabana and their adventure in Chinatown.

"Study it, there will be a quiz later," Balthazar said, sounding every bit the strict professor.

Dave considered the massive book. There was a *lot* to learn from the looks of it.

"Before we can put Horvath back inside the Grimhold, we must first turn you into a sorcerer," Balthazar continued. "Which begins now. Step back."

"Don't we stretch or something?" Dave joked.

Balthazar gave him a stern look. "Step back. Eyes open."

Dave went to say something but Balthazar interrupted him. "Mouth closed."

Dave wisely decided to do as he was told.

Balthazar stepped to the middle of the room. He held out his hands and they trembled. Suddenly, the concrete floor began to shift and undulate, finally forming a large circle. Dave gulped as alchemical symbols began to appear and mark off seven separate areas.

"This is the Merlin Circle," Balthazar explained. "It focuses your power. Helps you master new spells. It is where you will learn to become a sorcerer."

Balthazar stepped into the circle, and a glow seemed to light up around him. For a moment Dave saw the man's immense power. "This demands nothing less than total dedication," he continued. "Step inside, you leave everything else behind. Once you enter, there's no going back."

"So, I should probably go pee now?" Dave asked.

Balthazar shot him a look. This was no joking matter.

"I can hold it," Dave said as he stepped to the edge of the circle. A pulse of energy glowed from his ring and he nodded that he was ready. Balthazar returned the nod and began the ceremony.

"I am Balthazar Blake, sorcerer of the seven hundred and seventy-seventh degree. And you are my apprentice."

Dave couldn't resist the urge to smile. "Cool." He stepped into the circle and Balthazar began to prowl around it.

"Your ring is not a piece of jewelry," he commanded. "It's a connection to the sorcerers who came before you. It projects the electrical energy of your nervous system into the physical world. Without his ring, a sorcerer is powerless."

The great Merlinean sorcerer Balthazar Blake must find the one destined to inherit Merlin's ring.

"Take me up. Cast me away." With those words,
Dave and Balthazar become unlikely partners.

Balthazar and his archenemy, Maxim Horvath,
battle over the Grimhold.

College student Dave Stutler is more
interested in science than science fiction.

Dave's dream has finally come true—his crush,
Becky, has come back into his life.

After being trapped in an urn for ten years,
Balthazar is back in New York City.

Maxim Horvath will do everything in
his power to free his master, Morgana.

Sun Lok has some unfinished business
with a certain do-gooding sorcerer.

The Encantus holds both magical spells
and the history of sorcery.

Horvath recruits the help of the world's premiere magician— Morganian-turned-showman Drake Stone.

When Dave uses a spell to cut corners, mops and brooms come to life, causing total chaos.

The time has come for Balthazar to tell his apprentice the truth about his past.

Can Dave's newly acquired skills stand up to dark magic?

"So don't lose it," Dave reminded himself.

Balthazar nodded. "Only other thing a sorcerer needs is a nice pair of shoes."

Dave looked down at his sneakers and gave Balthazar a what's-wrong-with-these? shrug.

"Rubber soles block your current," he explained as he tossed Dave a pair of wing-tipped shoes that looked like something an old man or a movie gangster would wear. "Plus, it helps to look classy."

Dave turned up his nose. "These are old-guy shoes."

"Excuse me," Balthazar said, clearing his throat.

Dave saw that he was wearing an identical pair and quickly changed his tune. "I love them," he said.

Candelario worked as a cook in a grimy diner off 163rd Street. He was at work in the kitchen when he noticed a pot of water beginning to boil. Normally not a big deal, but this pot was not on a stove. It was sitting on a counter.

He turned and looked into a dark corner. Someone was standing in the shadows.

"Your father kept the list."

Candelario eyed him suspiciously. "Don't know what you're talking about."

"He was a civilian facilitator for Morganian sorcerers," the man said as he stepped out into the light and revealed his face. "And I'm Maxim Horvath."

Candelario's eyes went to the cane. He quickly signaled to his boss that he was going to take a break and headed out the back door to the alley.

"Haven't seen that cane since I was a boy," the cook said once the door shut behind them. "You been locked up a long time."

Horvath nodded. "Now I'm out. And I need soldiers."

Candelario shook his head. Things had changed greatly during the time Horvath was gone. "Whole thing unraveled once you went away. Know one kid who's a Morganian. Got a ring. But he ain't old school."

This was *not* what Horvath wanted to hear.

CHAPTER SIX

Dave was in the middle of sorcerer boot camp. He felt he'd been there for years. As Balthazar barked out questions, Dave tried to use telekinetic powers to move a pair of chairs in small circles. It was a struggle.

"If a sorcerer's molecular grip is weak . . ."

"His magic is weak!" Dave responded.

"First rule of sorcery?"

"Magic is not to be used for personal gain or shortcuts," Dave answered.

Exhausted, he decided to take a break and plopped down on one of the chairs. Then he noticed the time.

"You know what?" Dave said, standing up. "There's something I have to do."

Balthazar couldn't believe it. They were finally making progress. Before he could say anything, Dave headed out the door.

"I'll be right back," he called over his shoulder. "There's stuff in the fridge if you want something . . . really old to eat."

It was early evening, and Becky Barnes had just finished her afternoon radio show. When she walked out of the station, Dave was waiting for her.

"Hey Becky," he said as he fell into step with her. "I was listening to your show."

Becky smiled. "What'd you think?"

"It was amazing. I've never actually heard of any of those bands, probably a good indicator they're cool."

Becky liked that Dave was honest. Most guys wouldn't have said that. He walked her to the subway station. It felt comfortable. But suddenly a man stepped out and blocked their way.

"Cash, jewelry, give it up." He looked at Becky's

wrist and smiled. "Give me that bracelet."

Becky trembled as she pulled off her bracelet and handed it to him. Dave emptied his wallet, which only had eleven dollars in it. The man snatched it and shoved past them as he ran off.

Becky was scared and angry. "That was my grandmother's bracelet."

Dave didn't hesitate. His adrenaline racing, he took off and chased after the mugger. As he ran, he pulled the ring from his pocket and slid it onto his finger.

"Just give me the bracelet back," Dave said when he managed to catch up to the thug in a dead-end alley. "Please."

"Please?" the man laughed. "Run back to your girlfriend before you get messed up."

"Give me the bracelet back!" Dave repeated.

The crook shoved him up against the wall, and Dave gasped for air. He looked for any type of help and saw a large metal garbage can. Dave concentrated as hard as he could, and the can started to float in the air, wobbling slightly.

"What are you doing?" asked the man.

When Dave didn't answer, the crook turned around. His eyes grew wide. The garbage can was floating right next to his head.

Dave still hadn't mastered the skill of controlling objects, so the can suddenly burst into flames.

"You seeing this, too?" the mugger asked, terrified.

"Yeah," Dave answered, frustrated. "I'm vibrating the molecules instead of moving them, I think."

"You're what?"

Dave didn't answer. Instead he slammed the flaming can right into the thief's head.

Just then, Becky came running around the corner, expecting the worst. But to her utter shock, she found Dave with the bracelet and the thief unconscious.

"How did you do that?" she asked as he handed the piece of jewelry to her.

Dave tried to come up with an excuse. "I do a lot of cardio boxing."

Becky shook her head but went with it. "Nice." How could she argue?

She had called the police, who quickly arrived and dragged the man away. Becky ignored them, studying

Dave. "Something about you seems different," she said after a while.

He smiled and lifted up his foot. "I got new shoes."

They went down the stairs. "This is me," Becky said, nodding toward the subway turnstile.

"So I was thinking," he offered, not wanting her to go, "I could help you with that midterm."

Becky smiled. "That would be cool."

"It's a date," he said. Then he cringed. "Not a date. Just a, you know, an appointment."

She nodded and ran to get on the train, waving good-bye as she disappeared into the dark tunnel.

Dave's happy moment was interrupted by a voice from behind.

"Love is a distraction." Balthazar's voice was icy. "Becoming a sorcerer requires focus."

Dave started to say something, but Balthazar waved him off.

"Come," he said. "We have work to do. You've got a lot to learn." Clearly Dave's little moment of heroism hadn't gone unnoticed—but it didn't seem to be appreciated by everyone.

CHAPTER SEVEN

There were two parts to Dave's training as a sorcerer's apprentice—the physical and the mental. He had to develop the skills of a sorcerer, but he also had to learn as much as possible about the history and realm of magic. And with so little time, he had to do them both at once. After his heroics in the alley, Balthazar and Dave went back to the lab and got to work.

His next lesson had to do with the different parts of the Merlin Circle, which was now a permanent fixture on the lab's floor. There were seven regions in all, and Balthazar pointed them out as he walked around it.

"The domains of Space-Time, Motion, Matter,

Elements, Transformation, Mind . . ."

He stopped when he reached the last domain.

"And that one?" Dave asked.

"That one started the sorcerer war," Balthazar said sadly. "The Forbidden Domain. Power of life and death itself. Merlin was the only one who could access its power. Morgana wanted to learn its secrets. Merlin refused, and she killed him."

Balthazar stopped for a moment as he silently remembered that ultimate betrayal.

"Merlin knew she wasn't ready for that much power," he added, his stoic face even harder to read than usual.

"So I'm guessing that's not in today's lesson plan?" Dave said, trying to lighten the mood.

Balthazar nodded. He couldn't dwell on the past. After more than a thousand years of looking, he had finally, he hoped, found Merlin's heir. They needed to keep practicing.

Dave had already learned about vibrating molecules, but now Balthazar wanted him to get control of the element. He had Dave make a fireball. Then he told him to throw it—at him.

"You're sure about this?" Dave asked.

"Just throw it already," Balthazar said impatiently.

Dave hurled the fireball at Balthazar.

"The best way to defend against fire?" Balthazar asked calmly as the fire came toward him. "Vacuum sphere." He threw a spell at the ball in midair.

The sphere surrounded the fireball and put it out.

"Your turn," he said as he conjured up a much bigger fireball.

"Wait," Dave said pleadingly.

Balthazar threw the fireball at Dave, who with no time to think about it, instinctively made a vacuum sphere of his own.

"I can do this stuff," he said proudly.

"There's a lot you don't know about yourself, Dave," Balthazar replied. "Merlin believed your strength as a man determines your strength as a sorcerer."

Dave looked at his unimpressive muscles and gulped.

Balthazar poked him right on the chest. "Your strength here."

"That's deep," Dave said.

"Yes, it is."

It was going to be a long night.

Dave woke up on the lab sofa with no idea what time it was. He had trained through the night and had the aches and pains to prove it. He looked around for Balthazar but found only a note that read, "Keep practicing." Checking his watch, he realized he had just enough time to get home, take a shower, and meet Becky for their first tutoring session.

Practice could wait.

Or so he thought. After he took his shower, he found Balthazar in the living room of his apartment.

"What are you doing here?" Dave asked.

"You must have me confused in your mind," he said. "It is I who should ask you that question. We have work to do."

Just then Bennett walked in from the kitchen and handed Balthazar a cup of coffee.

"Thanks, Bennett, you are the man," Balthazar said.

"Your uncle is a trip," Bennett told Dave.

"He's not my uncle," Dave said, shooting Balthazar a look.

"Whatever. I wish I had an uncle to teach me the card tricks this guy knows. I'd score early and often."

Balthazar turned to Dave and whispered. "That's the kind of breezy self-confidence you could use more of."

Dave didn't want to hear it. He had to meet Becky and was not about to be late. He waved and headed out the door, leaving his "uncle" and roommate behind.

He was supposed to meet Becky in a coffee shop outside Washington Square Park. Suddenly, Balthazar appeared in front of him on the sidewalk.

"So let me ask you something, Dave," he said. "These plans of yours. They more important than becoming a sorcerer in the battle of good versus evil?"

"Let me ask *you* something," Dave said, feeling a bit annoyed. "Don't you have friends? Family?"

"No and no."

"That's kind of sad," Dave said and continued walking.

"Tragic," Balthazar conceded. "Let's go train."

"Look, *you* may not have a life," Dave said. "But I'm trying to. And I never signed up for . . ." Dave stopped in midsentence. Balthazar had Bennett's dog. "Why is Tank here?"

"I'm borrowing him," Balthazar replied cryptically.

Dave shrugged. Just add it to the list of things that make no sense, he thought. He looked across the street at the coffee shop to see if Becky was already there.

"Look," he said, turning back to Balthazar. "I have this thing now. So if you don't mind?"

He started to walk away again, but Balthazar put a hand on his shoulder.

"This girl, don't you think she might already have other interests?"

Dave rolled his eyes. "Aren't you supposed to boost my confidence? Give me tools to succeed?"

Balthazar smirked. "Why chase girls when you can levitate?"

"Just give me half an hour," Dave said giving up. "I'll meet you back at the lab."

Balthazar thought about this, as though weighing

the truth of Dave's statement. Apparently deciding his apprentice would return, he reached into his coat and pulled out an amulet strung on a piece of twine. He handed it to Dave.

"Take this," he instructed. "It lets me know where you are at all times."

Dave took it and then hurried to the coffee shop, hoping for a few Balthazar-free minutes. The place was popular with NYU students because of its low prices and large tables, perfect for laying out textbooks. He found an empty table and took a seat. A few minutes later Becky came in, and they started studying.

Dave may not have had Bennett's "breezy self-confidence," but he had to admit, he was feeling more sure of himself. Probably because of the whole sorcery thing. But more than that, talking physics allowed him to be himself around Becky.

Not wanting to overwhelm her right off the bat, he started with something simple. He asked her to list three characteristics of an electromagnet.

Becky pursed her lips and fiddled with her hair. It was as if she was running through a mental list before answering. "A current-carrying wire produces a magnetic field. The field reverses with the current," she finally said.

He nodded along with her and waited for one last one.

"And . . . I can't remember," she said, shrugging. She smiled sweetly. "Two out of three isn't bad."

"Actually, two out of three is sixty-six percent, which is a D-plus," Dave said matter-of-factly. Oops. That wasn't smooth—or very nice.

She shot him a look.

"Okay," he said, trying to be more constructive. "Check me out."

He started turning on his seat. She had no idea what he was doing. So he started spinning around in faster circles.

"What is . . . that?" she asked.

"This is me giving you a hint."

She scrunched up her nose and then she smiled when she figured it out. "The electromagnetic field grows with each turn of the wire!"

"Little game I like to call physics charades," he said

as they traded high fives. "I do an amazing *particle ion*."

"Now that I'd like to see," she said, laughing.

Dave stood up and started bumping into the next table.

"I didn't mean literally," she teased as she took a sip from her mug. "This place is the best. I'm addicted to their mint tea."

"Hope it takes the edge off uncomfortable social interactions," Dave said, hoping he didn't sound too desperate.

Becky smiled. "Not really."

Things were quiet as Dave considered what to do next. Every time he'd had a chance with Becky, he had chickened out. This time he was determined to say what he really wanted to say, even if it meant she might reject him.

"Hey, Becky, can I show you something?"

She looked at him curiously.

"Nothing weird. Well, not *too* weird."

CHAPTER EIGHT

Drake Stone had it all.

A superstar in the world of illusionism, he lived in a penthouse apartment that had spectacular views of Central Park and Midtown. Paid for by the countless sold-out shows he did, it was decorated in a Gothic style that made it look like a castle. And fittingly, Drake lived like a king.

Life was *always* a party at Drake's. It was *always* filled with an entourage of people whose sole purpose was to tell Drake how great he was. And there was *always* someone waiting on him hand and foot.

Right now that someone was a manicurist, who carefully painted Drake's fingernails a glistening black.

"You're kidding, right?" a voice called out from behind. It was not a kind voice.

All eyes turned to see who dared speak that way to Drake Stone. Maxim Horvath stood in the doorway.

"Who are you?" Drake demanded.

Horvath ignored the question and strode through the penthouse like he owned it. He walked out on the balcony and looked out at the beautiful skyline.

"I've been away too long. Since 1929 to be precise. City's changed, less crime, less mayhem. Fewer murders." He shook his head as if these were bad things. Then he looked right at Drake and sneered. "And *this* is what passes for a Morganian."

Drake suddenly panicked. His eyes flickered to the man's top hat and then to his cane. He gulped.

"Maxim Horvath," he stammered. "I've heard of you. You were one smoking bad . . ."

Horvath silenced him with a raised hand and turned to the others. "Will you excuse us?"

They were more than happy to hurry out of the room. In a few moments, the two were alone.

"So you're an *entertainer*."

"I'm the premiere alt-illusionist bad boy," he boasted. "Five sold-out shows at the Garden plus pay-per-view back end."

Horvath was not impressed. This *thing* in front of him was not a showman—he was a Morganian. That was why he was successful, but the career was beneath him. "Do you think Morgana ever pulled a rabbit out of a hat?"

"Look, my master disappeared when I was fifteen. Vanished," Drake complained. "Left me with nothing but an Encantus and some prescription-grade abandonment issues. So I improvised."

"The time for improvisation is over," Horvath informed him. "Balthazar Blake has found the Prime Merlinean."

Drake turned to Horvath, a worried look on his face. Even if he'd been alone a while, he knew enough to be wary of Blake—and the Prime Merlinian. "He wears the ring?"

Horvath nodded.

"We'll wait till he's alone," he informed Drake.

* * *

The opposite of Drake Stone's penthouse—both in coolness and attitude—was Dave Stutler's lab. But it was here that Dave had brought Becky.

"What are those things?" she asked when they entered the main room.

"Tesla coils," Dave said proudly. "I've been using them to generate something called plasma. I was so caught up with that, I didn't notice something kind of beautiful."

Becky looked skeptical. "Beautiful, huh?"

Dave nodded and directed her to the safety cage. "You're going to want to step into my cage."

"Okay," Becky said with a laugh. "Definitely first time anyone's said *that* to me." Dave's heart began to beat a bit faster. It seemed like, maybe, just maybe, Becky was having . . . fun.

They both stepped into the cramped cage. Dave flipped a switch, and the room went dark. The only light was the glow of his laptop screen.

"When you said *nothing weird* . . ."

"Hang on," he promised her. "Enjoy the show."

Dave punched a button on his laptop, and suddenly huge bolts of electricity began to leap back and forth between the coils. As they did, the bolts crackled with music, a combination of classical and funk.

"How is this possible?"

"The coils fire at such a high frequency, the sparks create sound waves as they move through the air," Dave explained.

The tune changed again, into the song that he had heard Becky playing on the radio the night before.

"Cool song," she said, moving her head to the beat.

They enjoyed it for a while and then Dave hit a button, and the crackling died down and finally stopped. He flipped the lights back on.

"All that time I was working down here, the coils made these sounds," he said. "Two years they made their own . . . music. And I never noticed it—couldn't notice it—until I met you. Listened to your show, heard how you talked about music."

In all her life, no one had ever said anything like that to Becky.

"Sappy, huh?" he said.

Becky shook her head. "You are not what I expected, Dave Stutler."

Judging by the look on her face, he decided that was a good thing.

Dave was on cloud nine as he walked Becky from the lab to her yoga class.

"Look Becky, maybe we can get together again tomorrow," he said as they walked down the hall. "Not a date. I know you and that guy are sort of . . ." His voice drifted off as he remembered the guy from the radio station.

"Andre?" Becky asked. "No. We're not."

Dave smiled.

"Besides," she added. "He's lousy at physics charades."

Becky turned to go to the class. Then she stopped and looked back at him.

"Call it a date," she said. Turning, she hurried inside.

Dave was speechless. He couldn't believe how well it was all going for him. Stepping into a rest room, he went up to a sink and splashed a little water on his face. Just to make sure he wasn't dreaming.

But then a voice spoke and he instantly wished he *were* dreaming.

"So, *you're* the one," the voice said.

Dave looked up and saw that someone was standing at the next sink. He was leaning over and running the water. Dave couldn't get a good look at his face.

"Excuse me?"

"Prime Merlinean, huh?" The man scoffed. "You don't look like much."

"I'm not sure I know what you're talking about," Dave said.

The man turned to face him. It was Drake Stone.

"Cool," Drake said, "makes this easier."

With a flick of his wrist, Drake cast a spell that set off all the hand dryers. The room was instantly filled with the sound of their motors.

"Can't have anyone hearing your girly cries," Drake said, raising his own voice over them.

"I don't know who you are," Dave said, confused.

This caught Drake off guard. He was a star. "For real? You don't recognize me?"

"No," Dave said.

Drake tried to show off the signature smoldering

look that he used on all of his posters. Dave shrugged. Still nothing.

This only made Drake angrier. He grabbed Dave by the throat and slammed him against the wall. After holding him there for a moment, he turned and walked away. Dave remained pinned against the wall.

"You can't weigh more than a buck twenty," Drake scoffed. He pretended to cast a spell, just to see Dave flinch. He did. "Nice," Drake mocked. He released Dave from the wall.

"Go ahead, hit me with your best shot," the Morganian challenged. "Your strongest spell. Bring it."

Dave was flustered. He waved his hands at Drake, but nothing happened.

The Morganian just laughed at him.

"Enough, you idiot," a voice said. "Watch the door."

Dave's skin begin to crawl. He'd heard that voice before. It was Horvath.

"Hello, Dave. I imagine Balthazar's been filling that head of yours with his vast knowledge. The great Balthazar Blake. Big on rules, isn't he? Never really liked that about him."

Dave tried to make a run for it, but Horvath grabbed him with a spell. He motioned with his hand, and Dave was slowly pinned back against the tile wall.

"I'm going to kill you," he said to Dave. "Right here in this lousy bathroom. But before I get to that unpleasantness, you're going to tell me where the Grimhold is."

Dave didn't say a word, and Horvath moved closer.

"Where is she?!" he demanded.

"She?" Dave repeated.

A smile spread across Horvath's face. "He hasn't told you, has he? The truth about who's inside that doll?"

Dave's silence confirmed Horvath's observation.

"You've put your faith in the wrong man," he said. "All his drivel about good versus evil. This world is about two things, power and control. Whom you own. And deep down inside, whatever else he says, Balthazar knows that. Which is why he *lied* to you." Horvath studied him. "Have you ever loved anyone?"

Dave tried to look away, but Horvath had him pinned too tightly.

"Ah," he said savoring the information. "You're *in*

love *right now*. I can see it in your eyes. I wonder what you would do if you lost her. You'd be no better than the rest of us."

Horvath tightened his grip on Dave. "This can go slowly while you ponder all the warmth and laughter you're going to miss. Or it can go quick and painless."

He let Dave consider this option for a moment. "Where is the Grimhold?"

Dave looked at him, terrified but unwilling to help a dark sorcerer, despite the threats. "I don't know."

Horvath shook his head. "You're a bad liar, Dave."

"That's what I keep telling him."

Dave smiled as Horvath turned. Balthazar stood in the doorway holding Drake Stone three feet off the ground.

"But he's an apprentice, what are you going to do?" Balthazar continued. He nodded toward Drake. "Want your guy back?"

Balthazar threw Drake across the bathroom like a rag doll, his body slamming against the far wall.

Horvath tried to shoot a spell at Balthazar, but the Merlinean easily blocked it with another one. Then

Balthazar pressed his hand against one of the mirrors on the wall and sent energy rippling across it.

"Been a while since I've seen a Hungarian Mirror Trap," Horvath said with a chuckle.

"Guess I'm just old-fashioned," Balthazar responded.

The two struggled near the mirror, whose surface was now rippling and distorted, making it look like the surface of a lake. They tried to pull each other toward the glass.

While they struggled, Dave caught his breath just in time to see Drake getting back on his feet. Drake summoned his strength and fired a blast of energy.

"Balthazar! Behind you," Dave called out.

Just as the blast flew across the room, Balthazar turned so that Horvath was in line with the blast. He was hit right in the chest. This weakened Horvath just enough for Balthazar to get the upper hand in their battle. With apparent ease, he tossed Horvath into the mirror's rippling surface.

The room grew eerily quiet. Looking above the sinks, Dave's eyes nearly popped out of his head. Horvath was trapped—*inside* the mirror.

Then, with a casual flip of his hand, Balthazar finished the fight by slamming Stone into the wall . . . again. That taken care of, Balthazar grabbed Dave and hurried him out of the bathroom.

"Glad I gave you that amulet," he said as they rushed down the hall.

"Horvath was going to kill me," Dave said, still stunned by the turn of events.

"His moral compass doesn't exactly point north."

"How about yours?" Dave asked suspiciously.

Balthazar stopped and looked at him, unsure of what he was getting at.

"That other guy called me the *one*, the Prime Merlinean."

Balthazar didn't say anything.

"You have been lying to me. And I'm not going anywhere until you tell me the truth. *Who* is in the Grimhold?" his apprentice demanded.

Balthazar looked back toward the bathroom and then down the hall. They didn't have time for this. He had to tell him.

"Morgana."

CHAPTER NINE

The mood in the lab was intense as Balthazar walked Dave through the *full* history of the Merlineans and Morganians. "After killing Merlin, Morgana's power grew," he explained, flipping through the images in the Encantus to illustrate key events. "She was making preparations for something terrible when I discovered the Grimhold."

Balthazar took a deep breath, as if vividly seeing the event all over again. "We managed to lock her inside it."

Dave looked over at the table where the Grimhold was sitting. "So that thing contains the greatest evil that ever lived?"

Balthazar nodded solemnly. "She's in the last doll."

"What does this have to do with the Prime Merlinean?" Dave asked.

"Merlin had three apprentices, and I was one of them."

"*You* were *the* Merlin's apprentice?" Dave said in disbelief.

"On his deathbed, he cast a spell to keep us from aging until we found the sorcerer who would inherit his power." He looked at Dave for a moment before adding the next piece of information. "And his dragon ring."

Dave looked down at the ring on his finger, then back up at Balthazar, his eyes wide. "You mean me?"

Balthazar nodded. "You, Dave. Heir to the power of the greatest sorcerer who ever lived."

"Why me?"

"When you were growing up, ever feel like you were different from the other kids?" Balthazar asked.

"Sure." Who didn't? Dave wanted to add.

"That voice inside that said, *You don't fit in*, was

really telling you, *You're special*," Balthazar explained.

"According to Merlin," Balthazar went on, "the only one who will ever be able to destroy Morgana is the Prime Merlinean. Only he can finally bring peace."

"So, I'm supposed to save the world?" Dave stammered. "I'm not really sure I'm up for that."

"I believe in you," Balthazar told him. "But you have to as well."

Dave shook his head no. "Look, I'd like to help," he protested. "But back there, I totally choked. I failed."

"Unfortunately, you don't have a choice. They know who you are. Who you may become. The Morganians won't leave you alone." Balthazar stood up and walked over to the Grimhold.

His eyes were filled with something Dave couldn't quite place—loneliness maybe? Or relief? The sorcerer went on. "I've been looking for the Prime Merlinean, for you, for a thousand years. Fighting off Morganians, protecting that Grimhold. Waiting for you to set me free. I'm going to train you, then release Morgana from the Grimhold so you can destroy her once and for all. The war will be over. Man will be safe."

Balthazar looked into Dave's eyes. "That's what I need. I'm not asking."

Balthazar slid Dave a duffel bag filled with baseball equipment. It was time to take the training wheels off.

Moments later Dave was wearing a catcher's mask and chest protector and standing in the Merlin Circle while Balthazar walked around it, coaching him.

"Remember, your cleverness, ingenuity, and heart will always give you an advantage over Morganians," he told him. "They rely too much on the power of their magic and not enough on the strength of their character."

He stopped his pacing for a moment to deliver a crucial point. "Magic can't be everything. It can't be all you are. Never forget that, especially when you begin to handle more powerful spells."

Balthazar held out his hand, and suddenly the space above his palm began to glow. Electrons swirled into a sphere of hypercharged matter.

"You want to bring in the big guns, there's only one weapon of choice. A plasma bolt."

Balthazar hurled the glowing ball at the wall and it exploded. Dave smiled. He had spent years trying to make plasma with Tesla coils. Now he was learning how to do it with his bare hands.

Unfortunately, Balthazar made it look easier than it was. Dave practiced and practiced, but he could not master plasma bolts. First they were so small they were almost comical. Then, when he got them bigger, they were too hard to manage and control. Some died off in midthrow and others came back and hit him.

After a while, Dave cried uncle. He needed a break. Without bothering to ask, he sat down on one of the steps that led up and out of the lab. "How will I know when I'm it? The Prime Merlinean?" he asked.

Balthazar took Dave's ring from him and held it up so that he could see the inscription on the inside. Dave read it, just as he had ten years earlier when Balthazar first gave him the ring.

"'Take me up? Cast me away'?" Dave still had no idea what that meant.

"The Prime Merlinean is so powerful within, he doesn't need the ring to cast magic. When you can

95

do that," Balthazar explained, "you're ready to take on Morgana."

Dave could barely do the magic *with* the ring. He couldn't imagine trying it *without*. He looked over and saw Tank watching everything, a giant string of drool dangling from his mouth.

"What do you need Tank around for?" Dave asked as he strained to get back up on his feet.

Balthazar signaled to the table where he had been studying an ancient parchment. It was a drawing of two human figures with arrows drawn between them.

"Schematic for a fusion spell," he explained. "The physical merging of two souls into one body. I've been trying to get it for ages."

Dave looked at the dog. "And you need Tank?"

"Practice," Balthazar said. "Animals are much easier than humans. Plus I kind of like having him around."

"Hang on," Dave said, putting it all together. "You mean you're going to try to possess Tank?"

Balthazar looked over at the bulldog, who was in midyawn. "Yeah, I'm not sure it's the best idea either."

"Has anyone ever done it between people?"

Balthazar was quiet.

"I've only ever seen one sorcerer successfully pull off human fusion," he said softly.

Dave knew there was more to the story. But for now he didn't push.

Maxim Horvath strode confidently into the university's administration building. He had not been beaten. Knocked down a bit, but he had more than enough fight left in him. Scanning the clerks who manned the information booth, he found the perfect one—a bored student doing Internet searches and chatting online.

Horvath walked up to her and rapped the counter with his cane.

"If you're not too busy borrowing company time," he said brusquely, "there's a student failing one of my classes. I need his file."

The clerk looked up at him. "You're a professor in the . . ." She stopped in midsentence when she noticed the crystal on top of Horvath's cane. It was now glowing. In moments, she was completely under his spell. He could make her do whatever he wanted while no one else in the room suspected a thing.

Horvath waited for the trance to take full effect before answering, "Psychology department." Then he said his student's name—David Stutler.

Without hesitation, she logged on to her computer and searched for all of Dave Stutler's information. She found his grades, address, high school records, and then something that truly caught Horvath's attention—a line marked: REQUEST FOR PRIVATE STUDY LAB SPACE.

Next to the request was the address of Dave's underground lab.

Horvath smiled. This really was too easy.

Dave was exhausted. The training had been grueling. This was evidenced by the fact that his catcher's mask was dented and his chest protector was covered in scorch marks. *Coach* Balthazar, however, wasn't letting up.

"See the molecules in your hand," he barked from outside the Merlin Circle. "Find the electron and grab it."

Dave looked down at the electrons now swirling about his hand and muttered to himself. He concentrated, and they began to swirl even faster, but he couldn't control them. Soon they wobbled and started slamming into him.

"I can't do it," Dave exclaimed as he walked out of the Merlin Circle.

"You *can*. You're not *allowing* yourself to."

Dave kept walking and plopped into a chair, totally exhausted. Then he spotted a clock and realized what time it was.

"Becky," he blurted as he sat up straight. "I have to get ready." She was due to arrive at the lab any minute for their date!

"We're not done training," Balthazar reminded him.

Dave gave him a look. "Come on," he pleaded. "I've been waiting ten years for this. Do you have any idea what that's like?"

Balthazar thought about it for a moment. "You better come back focused," he said. "We need to start making progress." Balthazar headed for a back room to practice his fusion spell. He knew to leave the couple alone.

Dave looked around the lab and sighed. It was a total disaster area. The remnants of his unsuccessful attempts to master plasma bolts were strewn everywhere. He needed to clean up fast.

He dug around in a storage closet which was filled with mops and brooms. Then he had an idea. What if he could put his magic to work *for* him.

Moments later, Dave was standing in the center of the lab surrounded by six buckets and six mops, controlling each one with magic. The sounds of classical music filled the lab as the mops began to dance across the floor, cleaning it. Next he added a vacuum cleaner to the mix.

He checked the time. It was running out. Satisfied that the cleaning was going well, he hurried into the bathroom to wash up and brush his teeth. The cleaning supplies continued on their own.

Dave had just made a big mistake.

A few minutes later, Dave walked back into the lab to find total chaos. The mops were splashing water everywhere. The vacuum cleaner was going crazy. Spray bottles squirted soap on all of the electronic equipment. Instead of looking better, the place looked a thousand times worse!

He commanded the cleaning supplies to stop, but they ignored him. They had taken on a life of their own. He wrestled with a few mops but only got covered in water and soap. In desperation, he grabbed one and broke it in half. Both halves grew into complete and separate mops. He was outnumbered.

Just when he thought it couldn't get worse, there was a knock at the door. Dave took a breath and cracked the door open just a hair, enough to see out but keep Becky from seeing the chaos inside.

"Hey," Becky said with a smile.

"Hey, you," he replied.

She saw that he was sweating and looked rather dirty. His eyes were wild. He did not look remotely ready to go out on a date.

"You forgot, didn't you," she said, hurt.

"No, I didn't. I've had this unexpected result in one of my experiments." While he talked, one of the mops repeatedly whacked Dave in the back of the head.

"So you want to do this another time?" she asked.

"Give me a sec," he answered. He closed the door and threw a momentary screaming fit. He was angry at the entire world for messing up this one thing that meant so much to him. Once he was satisfied that he was done screaming, he cracked the door open again and looked out, trying to project calmness. "Yeah, I think that would be best. I'm really sorry."

"It's okay," Becky said softly. "I'll see you around."

The way she said it sounded much more permanent than Dave would have liked. He desperately wanted to say something, but nothing came to mind. There was no way to explain it all.

He slammed the door in frustration and pounded the wall. This caused one of the Tesla coils to crash to the floor.

It was officially and irrevocably a total disaster.

"You think this is a game, Dave?"

Dave looked up. Balthazar had returned.

"Magic isn't a toy, it's a responsibility," he reminded Dave. "No shortcuts."

"Oh, yeah," Dave blurted. "What rule is that? Eight, nine, or sixteen? I can't remember!"

Balthazar glared, but Dave didn't care. He had been pushed past his breaking point.

"What does it matter?" He continued to rant. "Who cares about rules when I can't even control a few mops?!"

Balthazar calmly said, "The stronger the man, the stronger the sorcerer."

"Great, more useless mottos!"

Now Balthazar was less calm. "Try another one on for size. Your ring is writing checks that you can't cash. You can't control your magic when you don't believe in yourself."

"Oh, yeah," Dave replied, not backing down. "Is that what you do?"

"What I do is not important."

"You have no friends. No life. I'm not even sure if you have feelings. You're just here to make my life a living hell!"

Balthazar's anger was rising. "You don't know anything about a living hell."

A nerve had been touched, and for a moment neither of them said a word. Balthazar looked at his apprentice and tried to remember had hard it had been when he studied under Merlin.

"You're making progress," he assured him, sounding calm again.

Dave took off the ring and focused on the chair he had moved during the first day of training. He tried and tried. Nothing happened.

"Look, I'm not it. I'm not the guy you're looking for. I'm not a hero. I'm sorry. I'm just a physics geek." Dave looked down at his shiny wing-tip shoes. "Who looks stupid in these," he added.

He took off the wing tips and put his old sneakers back on. Then he walked straight for the door, but Balthazar blocked his way.

"Let me go," Dave ordered.

Balthazar considered it and then made a decision. He stepped to the side and let Dave leave.

Dave made it out to the street and headed straight for the coffee shop where he had tutored Becky. He hoped she might be there. Maybe he could still salvage the date. He smiled when he got there and saw her buying her mint tea.

But then he saw Andre and a group of friends come over to her. She smiled and they joined her.

Dave was too late.

He turned and left, but as he walked away, Becky caught a glimpse of his reflection in the pastry case. She looked out and saw him walking away, a look of total sadness on his face. She wasn't sure what she should do, so she just watched him disappear from sight.

She wasn't the only one.

Another pair of eyes watched from the rooftop across the street. Unlike Becky's, those eyes *weren't* friendly.

CHAPTER TEN

Dave wanted a quiet place to think about everything that was happening. So he went back to the observation deck of the Chrysler Building, where Balthazar had first told him about magic and sorcery. He wished things could go back to the way they were before that night.

Dave slipped the ring off his finger and read the inscription. He thought about throwing it over the edge, when a sudden gust of wind blew by. A voice called out.

"Dave?"

He turned to see Becky.

"What are you doing here?"

"I saw you outside the coffee shop," she explained. "You looked more . . . *distressed* than usual."

"Wow," he said. "That bad?"

She smiled and tried to comfort him. "We go back to when we were what, like, ten?"

"Kindergarten, actually."

"You think one botched date's going to make me hate you forever?"

Dave managed to force a smile. "A friend brought me here once," he said, gesturing to the deck.

Becky was noticeably staying away from the railing. "The height doesn't bother you?"

Dave hadn't even realized how close to the edge he was. "It used to. Not so much anymore. You scared of heights?"

"We're all scared of something, right?"

Dave laughed. "Some of us are scared of a lot of things."

Becky stepped closer to the railing and took Dave's hand. "Wow," she said, looking out at the city.

"Yeah, wow," he replied, looking just at her.

"Remember when you drew King Kong on the

bus window and he lined up with the Empire State Building?" Becky said after a moment.

Dave was stunned. "You remember that?"

"It was cool," she said with a nod. "You saw the world your own way. Saw things other people didn't."

"I was trying to impress you," he admitted.

She laughed. "Well it worked. Not bad for a ten-year-old."

Dave shook his head.

"What?" she asked.

"Just noting the irony of my ten-year-old self being cooler than my twenty-year-old self."

She looked into his eyes. "From what I've seen, twenty-year-old Dave's all right."

"*All right* all right or *knock-your-socks-off* all right?" he asked hopefully.

Becky laughed. "Right now? Somewhere in the middle."

Dave looked at her standing in the nighttime glow of the city. "I need to do something before I say something totally awkward."

"What?"

He leaned toward her and kissed her. She kissed him back, as the city twinkled below them.

It was . . . magic.

A short time later, the door to the lab opened and Balthazar looked up to see Dave entering.

"I guess we should talk," Dave said.

Balthazar shook his head. "It's in the past. You know I'm not big on emotional breakthroughs."

"Good," Dave said. "Neither am I." As he spoke, he raised a hand. His nails were painted black.

Before Balthazar realized what was happening, 'Dave' transformed into Drake Stone and cast a spell on him.

Balthazar was stunned. When he went to fight back, a force grabbed him. It was Horvath, standing in the doorway, the crystal on his cane glowing brightly. The Morganian cast a spell on some wires and they tied themselves into a knot around Balthazar's wrists.

Balthazar couldn't move his hands at all. The best he could do was lift a finger high enough to cast a quick invisibility cloak over the Grimhold.

"You really have a weak spot for that boy," Horvath taunted. "Has Balthazar made a friend?"

"I don't see the Grimhold," Drake said.

Horvath shook his head. "That's because you're using your eyes." He flashed a look at his enemy. "Clever Balthazar, always playing his little tricks."

Horvath lifted his cane, and the glowing crystal suddenly turned ashy black. Circles of smoke emanated from it and started to spread across the lab until they revealed the outline of the Grimhold.

Horvath smiled as he removed the invisibility spell.

Balthazar, meanwhile, was concentrating on the wires that bound his hands. He was trying to freeze them.

Horvath picked up the Grimhold. "It's lighter than I remember."

Now he flashed an evil smile as he took his cane and brought it down on Balthazar—hard. He did it again. And again. This wasn't just evil, this was personal.

"We once fought together, Maxim," Balthazar pleaded between blows.

"A lot's happened since those days."

"This isn't about *that*."

"Yes it is, Balthazar. It's always been about that. Because she chose you instead of me. The great Balthazar Blake."

Drake watched, confused, but pleased to be on the winning side. Balthazar was trying to stall; he needed a little more time. Frost now covered the wires, and they were almost brittle enough for him to break through.

"Now I'm going to let you watch me release Morgana," Horvath continued. "Let you watch your precious world crumble to nothing."

Using all his strength, Balthazar broke free from the wires. He knocked Horvath across the lab, but he'd forgotten Drake. The other sorcerer threw a plasma bolt that stunned Balthazar.

As Horvath kicked opened the side door to escape, he cast a spell and eight knives started flying across the lab at Balthazar. Their paths wove in a twisting storm as they flew through the air.

Moving in a blur, Balthazar picked them off one by one. But he didn't have enough time for all of them and only managed to stop seven. The eighth was headed right for him.

But it stopped inches from his face.

It hung in the air for a moment and then clanged harmlessly as it hit the ground.

Balthazar turned to the door to see Dave, his hands extended and the ring aglow.

"Nice catch."

Dave smiled. "I owed you."

But he was still too late. Balthazar and Dave rushed to street level. They burst through the front door in time to see Horvath and Drake race away in Drake's SUV. They were gone—with the Grimhold.

With a wave of his hand, Balthazar brought the Phantom's engine to life. They hopped in and chased after the duo.

"Horvath was a Merlinean?" Dave asked as they blasted through traffic.

"You heard us?" Balthazar asked.

Dave nodded. "He was one of Merlin's three apprentices, wasn't he?"

Balthazar sighed. "He was my best friend, but now

he's a Morganian and he has the Grimhold. I'm going to get it back."

Balthazar wove through the busy city traffic, quickly gaining on the SUV. Suddenly, Dave heard a whimper. He looked down and saw a terrified Tank. He picked him up and placed him on his lap. "Hold on, boy." This was going to get rough.

For a while, they had no trouble following Drake's SUV. But then it cut in front of a truck that was making a left turn. Balthazar, not quick enough, got stuck behind the truck. When he finally maneuvered around it, all that lay before them was a sea of identical yellow cabs!

"How'd he just . . . disappear?" Dave asked.

"He didn't," Balthazar said, shaking his head. "He's camouflaged. He's in here somewhere. Use your ring."

Dave looked down at his ring and thought for a minute. Finally, he raised his hand and pointed to the mass of cabs. He concentrated.

In one of the cabs sat Drake and Horvath, snickering as they slowly made their getaway. But then out of nowhere, the Grimhold that Horvath was holding began to shake and wiggle. It jerked free and smacked Drake right in the head!

"There!" Dave cried, seeing Horvath and Drake's cab swerving.

The Phantom raced through the mass of cabs, pulling up right next to Horvath. The two sorcerers came eye to eye as centuries of bad blood pulsed through their bodies. Horvath smiled, put his arm out the window, and touched the roof of the cab. It began to ripple, molecules rearranging before their eyes. The ripples spread over the entire cab until it transformed into a Ferrari F430 that quickly raced away, leaving Balthazar and Dave in the dust. Balthazar's face grew intense.

"You may want to buckle up," he said as he placed his hand on the roof of the Phantom.

As Dave scrambled for the seat belt, Balthazar did his own magic, transforming the Phantom into a Mercedes McLaren.

"No . . . way . . ." Dave whispered.

Balthazar floored it, the supercharged V8 engine echoing through the streets of downtown Manhattan.

Looking over and seeing Dave and Tank hyperventilating, Balthazar calmly said, "Dave, I got a job for you. Find a classical station."

"What? Right now?" he asked, breathing heavily.

"Yes, please."

Dave began scanning for a classical station as the two exotic supercars raced into a tunnel. They swerved and wove their way through oncoming cars. Horvath's window opened and his cane slid out, glowing in the darkness. Black smoke swirled off the handle, growing thicker as it streamed behind the car. Soon the entire tunnel was filled with black smoke.

Balthazar and Dave could see the darkness coming toward them. "Smoke screen," he stated. "I knew there was a reason he drove into this tunnel."

"Then why'd you follow him into it?" Dave asked, panicking.

Balthazar rolled his eyes. "Because we're chasing him."

They raced through the smoke, trying to keep Horvath in sight. Suddenly Balthazar killed the headlights. Dave shot him a worried look.

"The lights were reflecting off the smoke," Balthazar declared. "This makes it easier to see."

As the taillights of distant cars glowed through the black smoke, Balthazar bobbed and weaved around them. Then, out of nowhere, a truck swerved from the opposite lane, almost hitting them.

"Or easier to *crash into*," Dave said sarcastically.

"Classical music, Dave!" Balthazar cried.

Finally, both cars flew out of the tunnel.

But they weren't out of danger yet. Down the street, directly in front of them, sat a building site where a crane was moving a huge piece of mirrored glass. Horvath switched lanes, and Balthazar pulled up alongside him. Another stare-down. Suddenly Horvath cranked his wheel and drifted around a right corner. Balthazar, too, drifted, taking the lane outside Horvath's. Then with a wave of his wrist, Horvath sent Balthazar's car right *into* the mirror!

The evil sorcerer snickered as he raced away. Then, he lifted his cane and fired a blast back at the mirror. It exploded into a million little pieces. His enemy was trapped.

Inside the car, Balthazar looked thoughtful. "Right is left, left is right," he said to himself. He cranked the wheel of the McLaren to the left, and the car went right. Dave looked around. Everything was backward! Street signs, building fronts, streets themselves—everything was completely reversed!

Dave turned to Balthazar and was about to freak out when the sorcerer calmly stopped him. "Yes, we drove through a mirror. We're trapped in a reverse world. Horvath's payback for the bathroom mirror. And *no*, it doesn't happen to me often, but it has happened before," Balthazar said. Dave tried asking again. "No, we won't die. As long as we get out of here soon," Balthazar finished.

Dave sat quietly for a few seconds and then turned to Balthazar.

"By driving out another mirror," Balthazar said before Dave could even speak. He decided to keep his mouth shut.

Up ahead, they could see the mirrored surface of a building. As Balthazar raced toward it, the mirror disintegrated!

Maybe not that one, Balthazar said to himself. With renewed determination, he gripped the wheel and accelerated down the street.

Horvath drove through traffic with his cane out the window and blasted mirror after mirror before Balthazar had a chance to get to them.

As Balthazar blazed down a street searching for a mirror, Dave noticed a reversed sign.

"Hey, hot dog spelled backward is 'god toh'," he said with excitement.

"That is a really helpful observation, Dave," Balthazar said, going even faster.

Dave continued. "Yeah! We could go for a coffee in the 'pohs eeffoc'."

Balthazar shot him a look. This was no time for jokes. They needed a mirror—and fast. Then Balthazar found one. Up ahead he spotted the two-story mirrored glass façade of an office building. His last chance.

"This is it," Balthazar said, gripping the wheel as he raced toward their exit from this backward world.

And then, the mirror shattered.

Horvath had beat them to it.

As the mirror up ahead crashed to the ground, Balthazar continued driving toward it. He had seen something that Horvath hadn't. Dangling above the two-story frame was a huge shard of glass. It began to wobble, and then it fell.

A terrified Dave turned to Balthazar. "You're not."

Balthazar floored it. He was . . .

The McLaren hit the massive shard of glass just before it crashed to the ground, and with a ripple of energy they passed right through it. They were now *back* in the real world racing down a normal street.

Within seconds, Balthazar had caught up to Horvath who had made his way to Times Square. They swerved in and out of the busy traffic that filled Forty-second Street.

"Hey, where's my music?" Balthazar asked Dave.

Annoyed, Dave finally found a station that suited Balthazar. Classical music filled the car. "Happy?"

"I'd prefer something orchestral."

Dave glared at Balthazar. Sorcerers, he thought. So picky.

Balthazar followed Horvath through a hard right-hand turn and suddenly came face to face with a New York City garbage truck! Horvath had transformed his sports car into the garbage truck and was now lifting a massive Dumpster with its front loader.

"Uh-oh," Balthazar said nervously. "Didn't see that coming . . ."

He threw his car into reverse and started racing down the street backward as the garbage truck pursued them, using the massive Dumpster like a sledgehammer. Balthazar stayed ahead, but barely. Finally, he exited the narrow street, spun the car around, and raced down Fifth Avenue.

Dave rolled down his window as Balthazar watched. "Dave?" he asked.

"I got an idea!" Dave shot back. He leaned out the window and reached one hand out toward Horvath's dump truck.

"Uh, Dave,"

"Zip it, okay?" Dave said over his shoulder. Then the car stuttered as the McLaren turned into . . . a beat-up clunker.

Dave's mouth hung open. "Oh, fudge."

"This was your *idea*?" Balthazar cried.

"Actually my concept was more to turn *them* into a beater," Dave stated. "But, uh . . . my bad."

Balthazar shook his head. Before he had a chance to say anything, the garbage truck slammed into them. The race was over.

Climbing out of the destroyed car, Balthazar and Dave noticed that the garbage truck's cab door was open. Empty. No Horvath. No Drake. No Grimhold. Looking around, Balthazar saw Horvath pushing his way through the crowd.

But Horvath had one more trick up his sleeve. In the middle of the crowd he gently touched a woman on the shoulder.

Moments later, when Balthazar reached the same woman, he stopped in his tracks. There was something about her that transfixed him. He grabbed her, but when she turned to face him, her face returned to normal.

"I'm sorry," he said. "I thought you were someone else."

"Get your eyes examined," the woman said before she stormed off.

Balthazar watched her go as if he were in a trance.

"Balthazar," Dave said. "Where's Horvath?"

He looked back at the crowd, but now there was no sign of Horvath or Stone. They had disappeared into a sea of people.

"What just happened? Who was *she*?" Dave asked. Then he remembered. He had seen her picture in his Encantus. "She was the third apprentice, wasn't she?"

Balthazar nodded. "Her name was Veronica."

CHAPTER ELEVEN

Discouraged, Balthazar and Dave returned to the lab. Then, because he owed his apprentice the complete truth, Balthazar opened the Encantus and found a page with a painting of the beautiful sorceress Veronica. He would tell her story—for the first time in a very long time.

"She came from a noble family. She ran away because she knew she was different. When Merlin found her, she was starving and half-dead. But she had the gift. For centuries, Veronica, Horvath, and I were the only thing standing between Morgana and man's destruction."

As he talked, Dave looked through the pages of the book. They were filled with images of the Sorcerers' War.

"We were on the run. Outnumbered. No one to depend on but each other."

Dave looked up at him. "And you fell for her."

Balthazar thought back to Veronica. "Yeah," he said softly. "I fell for her."

Suddenly, the images on the page came to life, and Dave was able to see the story as though he were there while it was happening.

Two hooded figures hurry through a crowded medieval marketplace. One of them stops and lowers her hood. It is Veronica. The other is Balthazar. He turns to make sure they are not being followed. They are not safe.

"Veronica," he says.

"I know," she replies. But she can't take her eyes off a stunning necklace that an artisan has for sale on his table.

He can tell how much she likes it. "It's beautiful," he says.

"A man is going to take that to his home," she says, imagining it. "And, after they finish dinner, before they go to bed, he'll give it to the woman he loves. She'll be surprised. Happy."

Balthazar studies her. "You don't think that will ever be us?"

"If we don't fight Morgana," she says, "then who will?"

She pulls her hood back on and they disappear into the crowd of people.

The Encantus returned to normal.

"She might not have looked it," Balthazar said. "But she was the toughest of the three of us. Horvath fell for her, too. He asked her to marry him, and she said no."

Balthazar turned the page to reveal an image of the Grimhold.

"We had planned to lock Morgana inside the Grimhold, but on the eve of that mission, Horvath betrayed us. Morgana was waiting," he continued. Balthazar pulled up his sleeve to reveal a long scar. "I took her first shot," he said, running his finger along it. "Was about to take another."

He turned the page again, and Dave saw a large image of the final confrontation with Morgana. In the picture, she is about to hurl a fireball at Balthazar.

"Veronica made a decision," he continued. "One we'd both have to live with for hundreds of years. Veronica took Morgana's soul."

"She's the one," Dave said. The fusion spell! It was starting to make sense. "The only one ever to do that?"

Balthazar nodded.

"But she wasn't as strong as Morgana. Morgana began to take over Veronica from the inside."

Dave saw a single tear form in the corner of Balthazar's eye. "I had no choice," he said. "Let Morgana overtake her and she dies . . ."

"Or?" Dave asked.

"Or lock her up."

Dave's eyes opened wide as he realized the full scope of what had happened.

"*She's* locked in the Grimhold," he said. "All these years, you've been carrying her around."

Balthazar's pain was visible. "I was going to give her this that night." From an old leather satchel, Balthazar pulled out the necklace that Veronica had so admired.

"I'm sorry," Dave said sincerely. He thought about all of it. About how much it would hurt him to lose Becky, about how much she meant to him, and about how much pain Balthazar must be feeling.

"I don't know how," Dave said, standing up straighter, "but I want to be that guy who believes in himself. I want to be the Prime Merlinean."

Balthazar studied him for a moment. The determination on Dave's face was new, almost confident. "What happened to you?"

Dave tried to play it nonchalant. "Nothing."

"You're still a bad liar," Balthazar said with a smile. "I'm glad she likes you. Surprised. But glad."

Dave looked down at the necklace and at Balthazar. "I want to do this. And I can't without your help."

The faintest hint of a smile came over Balthazar's face. "Put your *old-guy* shoes on, we've got work to do."

Dave switched shoes while Balthazar explained what they would have to do.

"Each shell of the Grimhold is stronger than the last," Balthazar said. There were two layers left. "The inner doll is the most secure prison ever devised. It will take Horvath a few hours to crack. That gives us not a lot of time to turn you into a sorcerer and get the Grimhold back."

They began training more intensely than before. Dave *had* to learn to defend himself from plasma bolts. It was his only chance for survival. To do that, he practiced fending off plasma charges generated by the Tesla coils. They were big and relentless.

He got zapped a lot, but he started to block a lot, too. Within an hour, Dave had it down cold. He blocked three straight zaps and then used the energy to form a plasma bolt of his own. He was so impressive, Balthazar applauded.

"If you like that," Dave said with a smile, "you'll love this."

He whipped the plasma bolt right at Balthazar and knocked him flat on his butt.

"Now *that* is funny."

Both of them laughed.

Dave was finally getting it.

* * *

Drake Stone entered his penthouse to find Horvath standing at the window looking out over Manhattan.

"They're in position?" Horvath asked.

Drake nodded. He had spent the previous few hours on the roofs of various skyscrapers adjusting satellite dishes.

"Chipped up my mani," he complained as he looked at the nick in his nail polish. "Which is not cool."

Horvath shook his head. "No, I don't imagine it is."

"Below that lies our next co-worker," he continued, gesturing at the Grimhold. "Remember the Salem witch trials? She's the little devil that started it all."

Horvath smiled at the memory. "Once she's out, we're at the Morgana shell. And unfortunately, even with my substantial gifts, charm, and chivalrous upbringing, it will take a lot more time and energy to crack it."

Drake seemed more interested in his chipped nail than the Grimhold. "So what are we going to do?"

"Ever hear of a parasite spell?" Horvath asked him. He could tell that Drake hadn't. "No, that's right. You're education is . . . lacking."

"I go more by instinct," Drake replied. "What feels right."

Horvath nodded. "Parasite spell is a nasty piece of business. Allows a sorcerer to steal the energy of another."

Drake nodded like he understood but then shook his head. "I'm confused."

Horvath smiled and lifted his cane. "Not for long, my boy." Then, without a moment's warning, he smashed the cane over Drake's head, knocking him unconscious.

He bent over Drake's body and stole the ring off his finger.

"You weren't really using it anyway," Horvath said as he slipped the ring onto his cane. It slid down until it touched the crystal handle, and then both the handle and the ring started to glow. Electricity began to rise from Drake's body and enter Horvath's.

He was getting stronger.

He picked up the Grimhold. On the outside was the image of a young girl dressed in Puritan clothes. This was Abigail Smith. Energy flowed through

Horvath's body into the outer layer. Soon, she would be out and able to help him.

Back in the lab, Balthazar watched carefully as Dave controlled a huge plasma bolt.

"You're ready," he said. Then he added, "And, if you're not, we have to leave now anyway."

Dave nodded and grabbed his jacket.

As he headed for the door, Balthazar reached into an inner pocket of his jacket and pulled out the necklace. He put it in Dave's Encantus and quickly wrote out a note:

Give this to Veronica.

He looked at the necklace for a moment and then hurried to catch up with Dave—and face the future—possibly for the last time.

CHAPTER TWELVE

Minutes later, Balthazar pulled up in front of Drake Stone's building. Before they got out of the car, he turned to Dave.

"Promise me, no matter what happens, if Morgana *does* get out, you'll do whatever it takes to destroy her."

Dave nodded.

"These are my last words of wisdom," Balthazar said. "I haven't told this nugget to anybody in a long, long time, so listen carefully."

Dave looked up at him and waited.

"I got nothing," Balthazar said finally. "Whatever happens here, you wear the old-guy shoes well."

Dave knew this was the closest he was going to

get to a compliment. "Let's do this!" he said, ready to go.

Horvath and the newly released Abigail Smith sat in the living room of Drake's penthouse, admiring the Grimhold. After all this time, they had finally reached the innermost doll.

"It's time to release Morgana," Abigail said, cackling with excitement. Despite her young age, she looked evil and capable of doing great harm.

Horvath raised his cane. "I'll give her your regards."

Abigail looked up. "What are you doing?"

"I know you were only out for a short time," he answered, hitting her over the head. "I hope your stay was pleasant."

It wasn't personal. Horvath needed more power to face what was to come. And, well, he wasn't big on good-byes either.

Balthazar and Dave strode confidently down the hall toward Stone's penthouse. When they reached the door, they shared one last look and nodded. It was time.

Balthazar cast a spell so that the massive door silently lifted off its hinges and hung suspended in the air. Then the door lowered gently to the floor without making a sound.

They slipped into the penthouse. "Let's find the Grimhold and be done with it," Balthazar said as they split up, Dave heading for the living room and Balthazar going down the hall toward the bedrooms.

Balthazar reached the first bedroom. All of the furniture had been pushed into the corners, and a large map of New York City hung on the wall. When he saw it, his eyes narrowed. A giant Merlin Circle had been drawn over the map.

"The rising," Balthazar said wearily as he stepped into the room to take a closer look.

His eyes went straight to the southern tip of Manhattan. It had been marked as the Forbidden Domain.

Unfortunately, he was so busy looking at the map that he didn't notice the Oriental rug on the floor. When he stepped on it to look still closer at the domain, he started to sink.

"Persian quick-rug," he blurted as he struggled to break free. But the more he struggled, the deeper he sank. He had fallen for Horvath's trap, and until he could figure a way out, Dave was all alone.

Dave slipped into the living room silently. He was relieved to see that no one was there and even more relieved when he spied the Grimhold on a table. He quickly rushed over and grabbed it. Then a voice called out to him.

"Dave?"

He turned to see Becky. Horvath was standing next to her, holding his cane to her head like a gun. Abigail had helped Horvath abduct Becky earlier. Luckily Becky hadn't met Abigail's fate—yet.

"Give me the doll," he hissed. "You can have the girl."

"Dave, what's going on?" Becky asked, terrified. "You know these people?"

"No, not really," he answered, wishing very much that that was true.

"No need to be rude," Horvath bellowed. "I have

tried to kill you on several occasions."

Dave ignored him. "It's okay," he said to Becky. "You're going to be . . ."

Horvath cut him off. "No, she's not! She's going to be ground into chunks and fed to the cat unless you give me the Grimhold."

Dave's eyes darted around the room—he was hoping to catch a glimpse of Balthazar.

"He's admiring the decor." Horvath laughed. "What will it be?

Dave looked at Becky. Tears streamed down her face. He walked over with the Grimhold.

"Take it," he said.

"And the ring," Horvath demanded.

Dave let out a deep sigh and slid the dragon ring off his finger and handed it to Horvath. His last hope of survival was now gone. But he could at least try to protect Becky. He grabbed her and pulled her close.

"Merlin's ring. It's been a long time since I've seen it this close," Horvath said, admiring it. Then he looked at Dave and Becky, his eyes wild with hate. He conjured up a plasma bolt and hurled it at them.

Dave pulled Becky behind a couch just in time.

Through the sound of his beating heart, he heard Balthazar running down the hall.

Horvath heard the footsteps, too. He was not about to wait around. Tipping his cane toward Dave, he ran for the door.

Balhazar had said the Prime Merlinean could throw a spell without the ring. Dave decided to give it a test. He jumped up and waved his hands at Horvath. Nothing happened. He tried again, but the result was the same. It was no use. He couldn't perform magic without the ring. He slumped back onto the couch, defeated.

"The Grimhold?" Balthazar asked when he reached the room. He saw Becky still trembling and instantly knew what had happened.

"I'm sorry," Dave said.

Balthazar came over to him and put a kindly hand on his shoulder. "Of all the domains in the Merlin Circle, love is the strongest. I would have done the same thing."

But Dave had more bad news. "He took my ring. I

tried to cast magic without it, but it didn't happen. I'm not the Prime Merlinean."

"You're a good apprentice, though."

Balthazar looked over at Becky and smiled. "Balthazar Blake. We usually tell people I'm his uncle, but I'm not really." He leaned over to Dave and whispered, "She is way out of your league, by the way."

Dave didn't understand. Why was Balthazar being so calm? Things were very, *very* bad. He watched as his mentor walked over to the wall and pulled off a mirror.

"What are you doing? Where are you going?"

"Bowling Green," he said calmly. "Horvath is going to let Morgana out. They're going to try to use the Forbidden Domain."

Dave did not like this. "You can't take on him *and* Morgana. That's not even possible."

"I have to try," he said as he took two samurai swords from a wall display.

"I'll come with you. I can help."

"Without any magic?" Balthazar asked. "I can't let you. I'm going alone." He headed for the balcony, Dave and Becky following. Outside, the stainless-steel eagle from the Chrysler Building waited. Balthazar stepped up onto the railing and turned back to them.

"No one knows how much time they have to be with the people that are the most important. Enjoy it," he said, before adding, "This isn't good-bye, Dave."

Balthazar jumped off the railing and onto the eagle's back. The shining bird reared its head, and they began flying toward Bowling Green.

"Was that . . . from the Chrysler Building?" Becky asked.

"Yeah," Dave answered. "He does that sometimes." Then he seemed to remember what had just happened. "You okay?" he asked, turning his full attention to her.

"No! I'm definitely anything but okay!"

"I'm sorry." He searched for the right words. "I wanted to explain. I just never knew how."

"Just tell me the truth."

He took a deep breath and then blurted it out. "The first thing you need to know is I'm a sorcerer. I can slow things down, speed them up. Lift stuff with my mind."

Her eyes opened wide. "This is all crazy."

"I know. You get used to it."

With a jolt, he realized he *had* gotten used to it. There was no doubt. He was a Merlinean, which meant it was his responsibility to help mankind. More importantly, he had to help Balthazar.

With renewed determination, Dave stepped into action. He called Bennett and told him to go to his lab and find his Encantus. "Look up anything to do with the Forbidden Domain."

Telling Bennett to call when he found something, Dave grabbed Becky's hand and raced downstairs. Balthazar's car was where they had left it. Dave was planning to take Becky home and then head to Bowling Green to help Balthazar. As they pulled away from the curb, Bennett called back from the lab. He had information. Dave put him on speakerphone.

"'When Maxim Horvath betrayed the Merlineans, he showed his loyalty to the dark sorceress by handing over Merlin's most secret spell,'" Bennett read.

He stopped reading and asked, "Your uncle wrote this? He's got a jacked-up imagination."

"Bennett, there is a time issue here," Dave said, trying not to sound too anxious. "What was the secret spell?"

Bennett flipped to the next page. "Here we go. Morgana planned to use Merlin's spell to raise the dead."

Dave was silent as he thought about the dangers that they faced.

Bennett continued reading. "'Morgana hoped to call forward all dead Morganian sorcerers to form an army no man or Merlinean could stop. With such power at her disposal, Morgana could complete her dark vision to fulfill sorcerers' rightful destiny as rulers over man.'"

"This is it," Becky said, interrupting Bennett. She was pointing to her apartment building. "You can drop me off here."

Dave parked the car. But he didn't make a move to open the door or say good-bye to Becky. He was deep in thought.

"Dave?" Bennett called over the phone.

Suddenly Dave remembered one of Balthazar's

lessons. "The Morganians are vulnerable because they rely too much on magic," he said aloud to himself.

Becky looked at him, confused.

"The rings on Horvath's cane," he said, his voice growing excited. "He took them to enhance his power. But it also makes him a better conductor."

"I have *no* idea what you're talking about."

It didn't matter. Dave had an idea. A very good idea.

"Bennett," he said into the phone. "Stay at my lab. There's something I need help with."

He ended the call and turned to Becky. "Morgana's basically going to end the world as we know it."

"Oh," Becky said. "Just that?"

"And I'm going to help Balthazar stop her," he said confidently.

Becky considered for a moment. Then she made a decision.

"I'm coming with you."

CHAPTER THIRTEEN

I t had all started in Bowling Green Park. And now that was where it would all end.

Having arrived at the park, Horvath set the doll on the ground and pointed his cane at it. The crystal handle glowed, feeding off the energy of the rings that Horvath had taken from Drake, Abigail, and Dave. It burned brighter and brighter.

"Now they rise," he commanded. He shot energy from the cane directly into the Grimhold. It started to grow and buckle outward until a female form tore its way out. Horvath was startled. He was expecting Morgana, but instead he saw Veronica, the woman who broke his heart.

"You're speaking to Morgana," the woman growled. "No need to look so pathetic."

"But . . . it's Veronica," he stammered, still taken with her beauty.

"The Merlinean pulled my life force into her," Morgana replied. "But I've taken control of her body."

Horvath nodded, still a bit shaken. "Seeing her face again is difficult."

"You'll have your revenge soon," Morgana promised him. "Her spirit is still alive. After I raise the circle, I'll destroy her."

"All is ready to finally complete our plans," Horvath promised her.

She flashed a wicked smile. "Show me where the Forbidden Domain will lie."

Unaware that Morgana had been released, Dave was outside his lab. Balthazar's car was parked on the curb, its hood opened to reveal a massive, gleaming engine. Bennett and Becky came out of the lab carrying armfuls of equipment. Dave thanked them and started rigging something up to the front of the car. As Balthazar had said, the worlds of science and magic were one.

Bennett reached into his pocket and pulled out the necklace and the note. "Found this after we hung up," he said. "It was inside that book."

Dave read the note and his eyes grew sad. "Balthazar's not planning on coming back."

Back in Bowling Green, Morgana had found a spot in the fountain in the middle of the park. Now she began to prepare. "I cannot cast the spell until the circle is complete and the Forbidden Domain surrounds me," she told Horvath.

"I'll stand guard during your trance."

She looked down and saw the Grimhold on the ground. "Destroy that thing. I never want to see it again."

Horvath bowed, and Morgana began chanting to herself in an ancient language. As she did, a fiery bolt of energy shot out and slammed into a skyscraper. It raced up the edge of the building toward the roof until it hit the satellite dish that Drake Stone had positioned earlier.

From the dish, the bolt shot across the sky to another building and another dish. As it continued racing across the sky from building to building, a massive Merlin Circle began to form over all of the city . . . just like the one on the map that Balthazar had found at Drake Stone's penthouse.

"No way," Dave said, looking out the windshield and seeing the fiery circle in the sky.

"What?" Becky asked, looking out and seeing nothing.

"That is one very big Merlin Circle," he said. "You don't see that?"

"See what, Dave?"

"I guess it's . . . a sorcerer thing. No offense."

"None taken," she said sincerely. "Whatever you're seeing, it's part of Morgana's plan?"

Dave nodded as he continued trying to keep one eye on the road and the other on the circle. "Satellite dishes are basically just reflector antennas. I think they're using the ones on top of these buildings to direct and amplify the electromagnetic energy of the circle."

Suddenly he slammed on the brakes. Looking up

at the roof of a nearby skyscraper, Dave saw that one of its antennas was in the circle.

"Becky, I kind of need you to go up there and turn the antenna to disrupt that signal."

"On the roof?" she replied. Didn't he remember? She was afraid of heights. Like, seriously afraid.

"At least the view should be nice," he offered lamely. He needed her to do this. "The dishes only work if they're pointing in the right direction. This one looks like it's facing downtown."

Becky took a deep breath and nodded.

"Soon as you're done," he said. "Get out of here. *Don't* come back to the park."

Becky opened the door but stopped to tell Dave one more thing: "You know that note you wrote me when we were ten?"

He nodded. It was sort of hard to forget: "'Friend or girlfriend.'"

"I checked *friend*." She looked down for a moment and then right at him. "I was wrong."

With that, she was gone.

* * *

With Morgana in her trance, Horvath went to destroy the Grimhold. A flash of his hand, and a fire started on the ground in front of him, white hot and raging. He smiled gleefully as he looked at the device that had been his prison for so long. He angrily hurled it toward the fire, but it froze in midair before flying off to the side.

Horvath turned, knowing he wasn't going to like what he saw. He was right. The Grimhold had flown right into Balthazar's hands.

"You think I'm going to let you lock up Morgana again?" Horvath asked with a hiss.

"No," Balthazar replied drily. "I imagine you'll take some persuading."

In a flash, he threw two plasma bolts—one at Horvath and the other at Morgana. He was certain Horvath couldn't stop both. But he was wrong. Without missing a beat, Horvath used his cane to hit one bolt and direct it right into the other, obliterating both in the process.

Balthazar was stunned.

"All these years it was pretty even between us,"

Horvath said. "Not anymore. I've acquired some new jewelry."

He held up his cane for Balthazar and rattled it to show off the additional rings. Then he sent a blast right into Balthazar, slamming him through the fence that surrounded the park and into the cars parked along the street.

Horvath whistled a tune and smiled. This was going to be so fun. Glancing around, his eyes landed on his next weapon. He snapped his cane toward the giant bull statue at the end of the park. With a roar, it came to life. It snorted ominously as it looked for its target and then settled on Balthazar, who was still woozy from slamming through the fence.

"Did you know it can take matadors who've been gored by a bull up to three days to die?" Horvath cackled. "Sounds unpleasant, doesn't it?"

Balthazar scrambled to protect himself. The bull charged. Despite casting numerous spells, he was having a hard time defeating the creature. Finally, he was able to turn the bull back into a statue.

Horvath didn't seem concerned. "The circle's

almost finished," he said gleefully. "Then no more Merlinean drivel about serving man. Let him clean my shoes and beg for scraps as he should." Horvath raised his cane and started to generate a massive energy bolt. "Must feel rotten, Balthazar," he continued. "All those years fighting to stop this moment, and you came up just a little bit short."

But as Horvath was about to hurl the bolt, they heard a familiar sound.

Both turned to see Dave, driving Balthazar's car, racing down Broadway right at them. Horvath raised his cane, but inside the car, Dave just smiled. Horvath was in for a big surprise. Dave had rigged a giant Tesla coil to the Phantom. Flipping a switch, it pulsated with electricity. When Horvath raised his cane, the coil acted just as Dave had predicted. It became a massive electrical conductor. A blast of electricity slammed into the cane and flowed into Horvath, sending him to the ground.

He got up to respond, but Balthazar was ready and hit him with a flurry of bolts that knocked him out cold.

Balthazar loomed over Horvath. "Hard to see that one coming, huh?"

The tide was turning in the Merlineans' favor. The energy began reversing. Rather than flow from Morgana, it slammed into her and knocked her unconscious. Balthazar raced to her side, unsure if she was now Morgana or Veronica.

It didn't matter. "They're alive," Balthazar said to Dave.

As Dave looked on, Balthazar attempted the fusion spell he had been practicing. Slowly, he began to pull Morgana's spirit out of Veronica's body. Once it was fully clear, Veronica woke up. It had worked!

"You're free, my love," Balthazar said to her.

"What's happened? Where is she?" Veronica asked.

"She's gone."

Veronica frowned. "Balthazar, what have you done?"

He smiled lovingly. "What you did for me," he replied as his body began to contort and twist in pain. He had made the ultimate sacrifice and put Morgana's spirit into his own body. His eyes began to flicker with her evil energy as she tried to take command of his body.

"Remember your promise," he said, turning to Dave, his voice straining. "Whatever it takes to destroy Morgana." He held the Grimhold out for Dave to take.

"I'm not locking you in there," Dave said.

"I can't hold her much longer," Balthazar protested.

Suddenly, Veronica blasted the Grimhold from Balthazar's hand. "We'll fight her together."

Then Balthazar's eyes rolled back. When they looked back they obviously belonged to Morgana. She had full control of his body.

"How sweet," Morgana's voice said, looking at Veronica. Then she screamed and ripped her spirit out of Balthazar. She was free—and once again in her own body.

"Good-bye, Merlineans," she screeched. She threw a torrent of fire right at them.

"No!" Balthazar screamed as they braced for impact.

But it never came. The fire went around them—

they were protected by a vacuum sphere.

All eyes turned. Dave was straining with all of his strength to hold the vacuum sphere in place until the fire was gone.

"It *is* you," Balthazar said, stunned.

"Balthazar, you found him," Veronica said.

Dave had acted simply on instinct. It was only afterward that he remembered he was not wearing a ring. That could mean only one thing.

"The Prime Merlinean!" Morgana shrieked as she moved to confront him.

Dave's eyes opened wide when he saw the giant plasma bolt she conjured. He stepped back and she laughed.

"You have Merlin's powers but not his strength nor his skill. You're still weak."

"He's not alone," Balthazar said as he took his place next to Dave.

"You fool," she said as she hurled a bolt that ripped through Balthazar and knocked him to the ground.

Next Morgana focused on Veronica. She pressed her finger into the ground and sent a plasma ball under the surface. Dave had no idea how to stop it. It shot out of the ground and was about to hit Veronica when a bolt from nowhere knocked it off course.

It was from Horvath. His love for Veronica was stronger than his devotion to Morgana. "Somehow, in the end, it didn't seem appropriate," he said sadly. Then he collapsed, drained.

Dave moved toward Morgana, his eyes blazing.

She threw a plasma ball at him, and he didn't try to deflect it. Instead, he threw a temporal displacement spell at it, merging his plasma with hers.

The energy swirled between them until it reversed back toward Morgana and sent her flying through the air. She slammed into the ground, the plasma surrounding her. As the others watched, she appeared to almost melt into the plasma. Finally, she vanished into thin air.

For a moment, there was nothing but silence. The survivors were all too stunned. Then Dave let out a whoop. "No way," he shouted. "Did you see that, Balthazar?!"

There was no answer. He turned and saw that

Veronica was leaning over Balthazar's lifeless body. She looked up at Dave. "He's gone," she whispered.

"He can't be."

Veronica took Dave's hand. "Balthazar searched a thousand years for the Prime Merlinean. He died knowing he found you. Knowing he completed his quest."

"That's not good enough," he answered.

He looked around the park and then he remembered something important. "'The power over life and death itself,'" he said repeating what Balthazar had said to him. He began to pull Balthazar's body.

"What are you doing?" Veronica asked.

"If Morgana could use it to raise the dead, I can use it for Balthazar!" Dave said.

Veronica realized what he meant. The park was still part of the Merlin Circle. "The Forbidden Domain."

Dave nodded. He closed his eyes and summoned all the knowledge Balthazar had given him, all the power he inherited from Merlin, all the goodness within his soul. A fiery energy erupted from the domain and rose into Dave. The energy that Morgana had drawn was dark and frightening, but this was bright and full of life. He placed his hands over Balthazar's heart and put the energy into him.

"You and your stupid shoes and your rules and your following me around and your always saving me with that look on your face. You are *not* going to die!"

Balthazar's body began to shudder.

"Come on." Dave pleaded. You can't leave me now, he added silently. Or Veronica. There is too much here for you.

Suddenly, Balthazar's eyes opened and he started to cough, catching his breath.

Dave collapsed to his knees, exhausted—but happy.

"That took you a really long time," Balthazar joked, when he could finally speak. "I had this dream that you were insulting me repeatedly."

They shared a smile and Dave remembered something. He reached into his pocket and pulled out the necklace.

"I'm no expert," he said, handing it to him, "but I thought you'd want to give it to her yourself."

"Thank you."

Balthazar got up and Veronica ran into his arms. They embraced.

"Remember," he said, when they finally pulled apart. "You saw this once?" he held up the necklace.

"At the market," Veronica said, her face flooded with emotion.

"I was going to give it to you that night."

She pulled back her hair, and he put it around her neck.

"My Balthazar," she said quietly as they embraced again.

Dave watched, a rush of joy filling him. This was how it was meant to end.

Suddenly, a voice called out "Dave?"

He turned to see Becky. She ran to him. For a moment they just looked at each other. Then, finally, they kissed.

Dave had been wrong. *This* was how it was supposed to end.